Knowledge Keepers

Claudiu Murgan

Also by Claudiu Murgan

The Decadence of Our Souls

Water Entanglement

Crystal Cloud

Love Letters to Water (anthology)

Copyright © Everly Books Publishing Group 2024

ISBN Paperback: 978-1-7381895-7-1

ISBN Ebook: 978-1-7381895-8-8

C.S. Douglas - Editor-in-Chief, Every Books Publishing Group

Contents

1. The Bridge Within and Without   1
2. Seedlings for a Near Future   9
3. Ancestral Roots   21
4. Knowledge Keepers   31
5. Water Confessions   47
6. The Reset   59
7. Fibonacci Gamble   63
8. Crystal Continuum   83
9. The Story of the Seven Lakes   95
10. Streams of Consciousness   99

About the Author   105

Chapter 1

The Bridge Within and Without

"The rules have changed since we landed seven years ago, and we haven't come across anyone who's recently arrived yet," Dragos said to Lucian. He grimaced, unable to accept the lack of news from Canada.

"Can you ask a government official?" Lucian pushed back, pressured by the fast-approaching departure date.

Dragos sent further encouragement over the video connection. "You're better off going to the consulate in Bucharest. They should already have a document highlighting what to expect after you land. Don't forget that I'll be outside waiting for you, Lidia, and the kids."

Lucian pursed his lips as if just having tasted cold coffee. He knew his friend meant well and that he'd be there for his family to guide them through the maze of their new life away from home.

"Everything they have was included in the immigration package we got last month. It was very thin. Lidia's tense now that we're on our last legs before we say our goodbyes. I want to put her at ease."

No additional justification for the information he needed would make it materialize, but justify he did. It helped, like an item checked off on a to-do list might help release the bottled-up pressure.

Political, financial, and environmental challenges had entangled the world in a mesh of uncertainty and razor-thin stability, negatively affecting immigration rules in accepting countries, Canada included. His enquiry would reveal what —other than finding a job and being a model citizen—the government expected from newcomers. He wanted to contribute in a way that benefitted not only the Romanian community but society as a whole. Lucian's high sense of connectivity with Gaia and the ecological disaster for which humanity had set her up gave him an uncomfortable feeling of foreboding. Leading focused initiatives against river pollution, illegal waste management dumping, and irresponsible deforestation had turned his otherwise introverted character into a public figure. It also had the potential to make him a target of the corporations threatened by the influence his group of volunteers had on politicians.

"You've passed all the local interviews, obtained clean medical records, and were accepted; there's nothing else to be concerned about. Don't expect the encounter with the border officer here, in Toronto, to be more than a formality."

Dragos sipped from a white mug with the words "Tim Hortons" written on it in red.

Lucian knew he should let his friend go to sleep as it was past midnight in Canada. His worries had to stay his for the time being. He had read in the Canadian press about their own environmental challenges and the entities fighting to shed light on them and prevent future disasters. Somehow, he had the innate feeling he would have more of an impact in his adopted country. At least, that was how he interpreted his involuntary shamanic journeys.

"Talk to you soon," he said before disconnecting the Skype call.

Lucian's breathing slowed as he approached his Master Teacher and Cherokee father. He placed the thin wool carpets on the strikingly green grass, still kissed by the morning dew. On the carpet, he laid the tobacco pipes, a bowl of blueberries, and a bag of smoked deer meat—these were his offerings for the guidance he was about to receive as required by shamanic custom.

His sacred garden, a place of quietude he'd created through extensive mental practice, was still but for the three men, himself included. Lucian bowed three times in front of each of the elders, acutely aware of the precision of each of his movements, and recited an internal prayer of gratitude.

Enhanced by the lack of disturbing thoughts and noise, his senses welcomed the smell of cherry blossoms and lilac he'd added to his imaginary garden only days before.

Lucian straightened his back, eagerly awaiting the blessings from the men in front of him. On first impression, they might be mistaken for brothers. They had the same creased, pinewood-coloured skin, and the same black eyes in which Lucian always had the impression he could see constellations, comets, and cosmic activity he did not, as of yet, understand. Only the cut of their hair gave them their distinct looks: one kept it gathered in a ponytail reaching his middle back while the other preferred to wear his loose, cascading over his broad shoulders like a gray blanket specked with strands of light brown.

They chanted in a low voice over the background of a small, deer-hide drum that had materialized in his Cherokee father's hands.

The Master Teacher lit one of the pipes and inhaled as if to allow the smoke into every cell in his body. His exhale seemed to convert the smoke into ephemeral characters in a

story Lucian had yet to be told and did not yet understand.

His Cherokee father ceased drumming and chanting.

Lucian's gaze fixed on the elder's lips. "My son," he said, "today, we return your departed soul to you."

"Why did it leave me?" Lucian asked.

"Ignorance on your part. You forgot to nurture it and feed it meaningful thoughts, but a big journey is ahead of you, and your soul will be your inner compass."

"Canada?" Lucian mentally enquired, knowing his Cherokee father would pick up on his thoughts.

"Yes. It's a homecoming for you, my son. We have had so many broken bridges in this land of abundance. Steel your mind. Weather any storm that threatens your inner peace. Show others the connection we all have with Nature, as we are She."

The waves, trees, and a globe made of smoke hovering in the space between them dispersed with a sudden puff.

"In Canada, you'll meet people from many foreign lands. Be their bridge to understanding values of sanctity and appreciation for what has been given to us and what has been

protected and cherished by our ancestors." Lucian's Cherokee father's voice was hypnotizing. He ran his palm over his face to chase the drowsy feeling away.

"Lie on your back," the Master Teacher commanded.

Lucian did as instructed, his head closer to the elders, and the men blew gently on him. Lucian felt a jolt of energy and a higher perception of the details of his sacred garden.

Moments later, he returned to the real world—his bedroom in Bucharest—confident the spirit world would deliver further messages in preparation for the upcoming milestone in his family's life.

Dragos giggled loudly as soon as the video connection was up. "Three more days, buddy."

Lucian radiated excitement. Now and then, tinges of worry circled his strengthened mind, but a silent, mental calling to his invisible friends helped clear it. "Everything's packed, and I think everyone's ready for the flight," he replied. "This is our last face-to-face, my friend."

Dragos's wife, Doina, joined the discussion. "How's Lidia doing?"

"Hi, Doina. Much better, now that her father's recovered from the nasty cold he had. Our parents on both sides have made peace with our decision," Lucian clarified.

Doina pulled closer to Dragos and said, "It's not easy for any of us. I don't assume it was easier twenty or thirty years ago, either. We left behind the life we knew. It's embedded in our DNA. Now, we have to adjust mentally, physically, and psychologically. We have the option of keeping our spiritual side unchanged, though."

Lucian nodded and looked behind him to see if Lidia would join them, but she was still out of the picture.

"The kids will love it here. They'll adapt well and find their purpose in life without forgetting their roots," Doina continued, her voice little more than a whisper. "We're the ones who have to work harder at finding a purpose to keep us going."

Lucian noticed the gentle squeeze she gave Dragos's hand, like a renewed vow of her love for him. "We're here for you, and later on, you'll support others to smooth their path."

"Thank you," Lucian said. Maybe his job would give him the necessary drive, or maybe something unexpected would be the kicker. No matter. He'd go with the flow and trust his inner guidance, reflected in the ad-hoc journeys to his private realm.

He often asked himself how his voice might be heard in a multitude of nations. Was he so special that he should be heard at all? What was life? For Lucian, it was a succession of experiences one went through, consciously or not, learning from them or not. For others, life might represent a multitude of bridges over streams of happiness, elation, gratitude, love, delusion, deprivation, devastation, loneliness, or self-doubt. It might also be a web of paths, some rough, some smooth, some a combination of both.

The couple from Canada said, "Have a safe flight," before hanging up.

Lucian slid into his sacred garden, looking for answers and reassurance. Only his Cherokee father welcomed him this time. Together, they approached the banyan tree, a true force of Nature, as Buddha had millennia ago.

The men offered a short prayer to the ancestors, turning them into energy entities that became one with the trunk and were pushed along the trunk with the water and minerals. The branches grew thinner toward the top, and Lucian felt lighter when his unsubstantiated body was released from its wooden host.

"A required purification," his Cherokee father explained without looking at him.

They flew from his sacred place to a destination that had yet to be revealed, claiming the space between the ground and the celestial ceiling. Enthralled by the possibility of flight, Lucian gazed at the lights speckling the dark blue sky. He saw unique patterns in the abyss of his Cherokee father's eyes, the numerology of the universe in a fractal imprint.

"We are descending," the elder announced, and a sudden heaviness pulled Lucian down near a vast body of water. He couldn't avoid dipping beneath the surface, and he instinctively held his breath. His energy body adapted to the pressure; it was as if it had grown gills.

Submersed, the men treaded water as if waiting for something extraordinary to happen. The water trembled around them, clicking and whistling as if there were a waterfall in the distance. Light from above pierced the darkness, and Lucian made out even darker spots floating toward them.

"Whales!" The word exploded in his mind followed by a sliver of panic the likes of which he couldn't shake. "Our ancestors are here," the elder said, sensing Lucian's unease. "It is a great honour for us to meet them at this point in time. They think you could help them."

The group of whales surrounded them, each of them focusing a single eye on Lucian, scrutinizing him with intensity, and he was overwhelmed in the presence of such impressive, intelligent beings.

Lucian detected a thought form approaching, a beam of energy validated by all members of the group. "Turn the journey you are about to start into more than a personal experience. Consider yourself more than a speck in the timeless, infinite universe. Think of yourself as an endless well of love and gratitude with the ability to impact those who are frightened by global calamities and waiting on the sidelines.

"Express and expose the pain caused by those hunting us to fulfill our primary instincts.

"Be eloquent as you tell everyone about the breakdown of the ocean that has been our home on this globe since we arrived on Earth. The water is dying, and us along with it.

"Become the bridge of reason crossed by those in possession of a light heart and a purpose to serve.

"Your voyage through time and space will raise awareness in others, too."

A high-intensity whistle signalled for the pod of mammals to leave. They blinked at Lucian in unison, and he waved at them while his legs simulated the treading of water needed to keep him in place.

The Cherokee touched Lucian's shoulder and motioned for him to head for the surface, and the water formed a wave to push them gently toward the surface from where the men began the flight back.

They reached Lucian's sacred garden, where they were purified and blessed by the ancestors. Lucian waited patiently until his Cherokee father had selected the pipe and jar of honey from the offerings he'd given him.

Another cycle of his spiritual evolution concluded, Lucian's purpose in his adopted country having achieved confirmation.

(First published in the anthology Building Bridges by Immigrant Writers Association - 2019)

Chapter 2

Seedlings for a Near Future

The digital remote attached to his reclining chair burped a monotone sound, and the metallic voice of the AI monitoring the retirement facility talked to him. "Incoming call for Macek Nowak—do you accept it?"

He was staring at a six-by-nine-foot window, framing an excessively blue sky—a canvas for the passing clouds as they were handled by the high winds. When Macek squeezed his eyes to focus on the celestial imagery, he often had the impression that what he was seeing was nothing but an illusion projected onto a dome surrounding the entire neighbourhood of twenty buildings that hosted cranky, out-of-shape, slow-minded retirees.

His weak eyesight, which could have been improved with ocular surgery had his pension fund not fallen short, perceived the way the sky seemed to vibrate as an undulation of sorts, waves of energy mimicking the breath of the ocean.

When taken outside to the garden by the nurse-robot for his daily stroll, Macek would squeeze his eyes even tighter into a thin line into what amounted to a fuzzy, outdated telescope that was unable to identify the pixels on what he believed was an artificial sky.

The sizzling breeze was always the same, whether in direct sunlight or the shade of his favourite palm tree by the tiny pond edged with polished black stones. He sniffed the air many times like his dear Pockey, the beagle who had been his trusted companion, as he made his way through the winding forest trails. There was no scent of freshly cut grass, nor was there as much as a whiff of the milkweed and tickseed flowers that had been planted in convoluted patterns by the AI gardeners.

In fact, the weather didn't change much throughout the year. The color gradient of the flocks of clouds varied in their passing only with the quantity of mist that descended every now and then from the same, unchanging sky.

Macek switched the focus of his gaze to his own reflection in the window. He could only make out the bleached goatee and the sides of his straight cheeks. The rest of his oval face extended into a hairless, wrinkled top that melded with the glitter of the sun.

Even before he'd checked himself into the Jacksonville Retirement Facility five years ago, Macek—a former forester —had spent most of his adult life outdoors in the St. Lawrence Forest Region, caressing large gatherings of blue ash, walnut, and black gum scattered with white pine like uninvited guests at a private party. As a child, Macek cherished the stories his grandfather—a rough Polish man with a body like an oak that had pulled out its roots, ready to settle somewhere else—used to tell about the secular forests of the motherland. All of his life, Macek couldn't completely shake the feeling that his roots belonged in a different soil he'd never had the chance to visit. And now, in Florida, the perception of being a stranger in a strange land hung heavily over him.

Back in Ontario thirty years ago, Macek's experience with the dynamics of the woodland—the humidity in the air, the direction of the wind, and the health of the mature trees—would have predicted the daily weather, but not in ever-sunny Florida, where the Canadian government shipped all retirees over eighty years of age. It was the only place close to home that was able to provide decent, AI-assisted living on an affordable budget.

"Macek Nowak, will you accept the call?" the voice chimed again in the quietness of his room.

"Yes."

He had no close family members who might call him, or friends with enough clarity of mind to remember his exact coordinates.

The wall-mounted glass screen powered on, and a tiny, strikingly white face surrounded by an aura of unruly blonde hair came into focus.

"Hello, Mr. Nowak. I'm Susan Deerwalk, president of the Toronto District School Board."

Macek straightened his back in his chair and tried to mumble a hello, but before he could clear his throat to vocalize intelligible words, she continued: "The Board is assessing the opportunity to introduce several environmental programs into the curriculum in elementary schools across the province if you know what I mean." The woman's upper lip twitched, and she looked down as if searching for something she needed to carry out the discussion.

No, Macek did not know what she meant, but he kept his eyes on her, waiting for the details.

"It's called 'Seedlings for the Near Future.'" Susan Deerwalk smiled at him with her mouth only, the colour of her eyes staying hidden behind barely open slits.

It wasn't his near future or that of the kids, for that matter. Near or extended, the future would be bleak for the generations to come in their environmentally depleted, marketing-based, emotionless society.

"How can I help?" He hoped he came off as warm and open to the possibility. In truth, his energy was ignited by the thought of his dear trees.

"You were the last superintendent forester of the St. Lawrence Forest Region before its decimation by fire, twig beetles, and irresponsible logging, if you know what I mean." Her lip twitched again, and Macek couldn't say if it was the subject of trees that made her uncomfortable enough to generate the muscle spasms or a suppressed fear or anxiety she was unable to hide.

His face froze, and he couldn't control the welling of tears in his eyes.

Deerwalk's face stayed the course for the duration of her prepared speech, seemingly insensitive to Macek's reaction. "We'd like to think we have learned from the mistakes of previous generations if you know what I mean," she continued. "Along with the reforestation initiative, effectively doubling the two million hectares that are left of the initial area of twenty million, it is the educational component that requires your assistance."

She paused, but he kept silent, fearful he might bawl like a hungry baby destined to remain unconsoled as he had nothing more than a pacifier.

"This is a two-month, once-a-week virtual program. We'll schedule the trips on the weekday that works best for you if you know what I mean," Deerwalk continued. "For once, we don't want to record this material. You'll connect remotely via satellite while the children will be on the ground, following your instructions. It's up to you to select the trails, preferably easy terrain. "

He nodded and waited for more.

"The pristine environment in which these children grew up failed to instill strong immune systems in them, but we would like to slowly introduce them back to nature. Organizing field trips to the wilderness is risky, but we have received consent from parents and guardians."

She shook her head, the halo of her hair following in slow motion. "Air trips in small numbers have worked in the past for students whose parents could afford the cost. Now, the program will fund every child wanting this experience. We realize that we need to give them a real adventure so they will understand the essence of what's going on below the overstory if you know what I mean. That is what you call it, isn't it?"

Before he could say anything, she continued: "The virtual technology has passed its infancy in terms of replicating the smells and sounds of the forest."

Macek stared blankly at the woman and puffed nervously. Smells and sounds? How could she encapsulate the dynamics of an entire ecosystem in two words? The mature blue ash, slender and proud, oversaw and cheered for its upcoming relatives, the sap of its sap, as they pushed themselves toward the scarce light filtering through the overstory Deerwalk had mentioned as a noun without meaning on her tongue. Close to the forest floor were blue ash seedlings, always in danger of deer feeding on their tiny young leaves, leaving them naked and exposed to the heavy paws of a bear or the hasty passing of a pack of wolves. Trees spoke to one another, emitting sounds inaudible to the human ear. The leaves of the walnut and black gum trees, saturated with chlorophyll, screamed for joy in the form of the oxygen that had filled Macek's lungs when he was still doing his rounds deep in the bush when his encounters with the wildlife had brought him to a state of bliss he had yet to find since, even in his quietest moments.

"But it's the sense of touch, the feel of the rough bark and miniature cones being held by the students and the broken branches turned into walking sticks that we really want them to experience, and that can't be replicated yet," Deerwalk said. "Oh, and if they happen to get a small scratch, it won't be a problem—medical personnel will accompany them if you know what I mean."

Without knowing it, she had used keywords to trigger vivid imagery culled from the folders of Macek's memory, dusting them off like a forgotten childhood toy that had been thrown into a dark corner of the attic.

His fingers, gnarled by arthritis, closed painfully on the ends of the armrests.

Bark!

There had been so much disrespect in the way she'd pronounced the word "bark." No, it wasn't a fungible garment stapled to the oak, the birch, or the Douglas fir, you insensitive board president, he wanted to yell. The bark of the blue ash tree, like scales on the back of a dragon but not as smooth, came to mind. It stood between his eyesight and the image of the woman who wanted his help to give the next generation knowledge about a decimated habitat, things that, during his teenage and adult life, had been common sense.

Humanity tended to brand trees like cattle, not with a hot cauterizing iron but with blood-red paint to mark the healthiest and the tallest. He was sure the trees felt pain, knowing they were about to fall from their vantage points down to the moist soil they couldn't see from their point of view but from which the nutrients, water, and signals from their brothers and sisters had come.

Macek had witnessed the whimpers and moans of the towering Douglas firs firsthand, echoed by the birch throughout the woodland cathedral, with each fatidic X marking their bark. The trees had said their goodbyes to the world they had grown up in before being turned into a freshly cut stump, disfiguring the forest.

He pushed his fingers deeper into the fabric of the chair until he felt the metal frame and used it as a lightning rod to deflect his rage. Macek could sustain his smile no more, and the lines of his mouth and eyebrows formed arches in opposite directions.

"Look," Susan Deerwalk said, "it's not like you have a long daily To-Do list if you know what I mean." She winked at him like a juvenile trying to hook up with an older man.

The crass verbal blather manifested a pain in his chest. He nodded, but he wasn't sure why. Maybe it was a subconscious gesture deflecting some of the garbled vibrations radiating from Deerwalk, even through the glass screen.

Macek didn't have to close his eyes to enter the natural cathedral to which he'd spoken and prayed with reverence throughout his life as a forester. The feeling of being a part of the forest as a rare breed of walking tree never left him. He couldn't grow roots; he didn't want to. Roaming, observing, hugging, and caressing the beings that had manifested in all their wooden glory had much more meaning for him.

It had taken him years to silence his mind and remain still as he sat on a boulder, etching the sound of leaves being ruffled by the wind, the swing and crackle of a young tree trunk being pushed by a strong breeze, or the sound of the tug-of-war between the boisterous water and the silent stones into his mind. Later on, with practice, his senses were further enriched by the trills of the woodpecker, the loon, and the moose.

He said, "I'll do it on three conditions." His subconscious shuffled his legs on the laminate floor as if rubbing against the layers of pine needles, moss, twigs, and the crimson of the black gum leaves on the forest carpet. When softened by the passing rain, the ground's canvas—already decorated with pastels of greens, reds, and browns—held onto his footprints, adding to the exclusive work of art.

Susan Deerwalk gestured with her hands to indicate that she was listening.

"I won't live forever. You're lucky I still draw breath. Hire a young lad so I can pass my knowledge on to him at the same time and for as long as I wake up every darn morning."

"What's the second condition?" Macek expected the twitch again as she probably couldn't foresee any opposition from a decaying oak like him that had been hollowed out by fungus and voracious insects and dangerously inclined by tenacious winds while maintaining a level of dignity sustained by its dry, bare roots.

"You don't censor my language while I teach the kids. I'll tell them good, bad, sad, and happy stories. I'll tell them about how, numb from pain, I cried over the oozing wound of a three-hundred-year-old walnut. They made bookshelves and fancy kitchen tables out of him. An elder of the forest, cut down with stupid irresponsibility."

Macek let go of the armrests and stood up, blood sizzling through his thin, aged veins. "I'll show them where the spiders, centipedes, and solitary worms hide and how they panic in disarray when the students lift their protective layer of leaves with the end of their bent sticks."

Susan Deerwalk's twitch came and went fast, like a flash of anger flitting across the slits of her eyes.

"You said you wanted to show the kids authenticity," he said, his voice firm. "Let's give it to them. You can't get more authentic than me."

The woman stayed silent as if she had exhausted her vocabulary and was waiting for another download of words to counter Macek's conditions.

"Even from here, through the screen, I can lead them to the hollow trunk of pinewood with shredded edges and help them make sense of its decay. They will understand why it is important to keep fallen trees on the forest ground for nutrients if you know what I mean."

Her verbal tick had escaped his lips involuntarily, and he failed to refrain from the smile that sweetened her hardened facial expression. Macek suddenly comprehended how much he missed the forest. He would have given up his third condition until moments ago if Deerwalk had pushed back, but this realization only served to cement his will.

"And my third condition..." His voice trembled while the woman's shoulders tensed as if bracing for impact. "When I pass and join the Creator, I want this shell of a body to return to where it belongs. In the forest."

Susan Deerwalk gasped. Her eyes opened wide, finally showing their colour. They were the green of walnut shells, soft and kind. "How could I—"

He raised his hand, ceasing the unnecessary justification of her limited sway with the board.

"My life insurance will cover the shipping expenses for my coffin. I'll adjust my will so the leftover money will be donated to environmental programs in Ontario. You can use it to train more people and increase the number of children involved in your outdoor trips."

Tears burst from the corners of her eyes. She made no attempt to extinguish them.

"Generations have lost the meaning of nature. Let's rebuild it together properly."

He could teach them so many things. About the disfigurement of the land laid bare in deforested areas. About the black walnut, shagbark hickory, and sugar maple bargaining for resources in depleted patches. About Ontario's ecosystem, that still complied with the signals sent by the water, the air, the birds, and their cousins from across the oceans, sent via invisible threads of energy that humans were unable to sense or see.

"I'll help you raise your seedlings if you help me enrich the understory for the seedlings of my dear oaks, pines, and sugar maples," he said in a last-ditch effort.

Susan Deerwalk nodded, and then, with a shaky voice like a leaf enduring the blows of the spring wind, she whispered, "I personally promise you that you'll rest among the fallen, mighty trunks, where you can hear the quarrel of the leaves and inhale the scents of the forest."

Macek approved the statement with a sheepish smile. He had the assurance that his body would end his immigrant status so his soul could linger in the astral plain until its next assignment. He also noticed an added dram of respect in Deerwalk's tone when she mentioned the sounds and smells of his beloved, and he knew the teaching had already begun.

(First published in the anthology Grow Together by Immigrant Writers Association - 2020)

Knowledge Keepers

Chapter 3

Ancestral Roots

Rowana sat on a rough cotton rug striped with primary colours, her eyes closed, her palms resting on her crossed legs. The clearing in the forest, away from the beaten path and noise pollution of the city, called to her silently. It was a patch of grass like the eye of a giant, wide open and looking upward.

Around it, Douglas firs, proud and straight like a crowd of old English gentlemen, gathered at the country club mingled with wide and wise oaks whose trunks seemed to morph into wolves, bears, owls, and half-distorted human faces. They were the spirits haunting the forest and imprinting themselves in the ancient bark.

There was no smell or sound in the void created by her presence, but she sensed familiar energy entities hovering around the edges of the protective space and the tips of the trees.

The smouldering tobacco bundle appeared in her right hand. First, she inhaled the smoke, then, with her left hand, she moved it slowly over her head, under her arms, and around her legs. The purification was a part of her ancestral ritual, a ceremony that she now, as the only survivor of her tribe, had to perform by herself.

A gentle nudge of thought replaced the tobacco with a rattle, and the beat started on its own as if embedded in her subconscious. The rhythm brought trepidation to her body, wave after synchronized wave until her physical surroundings disappeared.

"Hey Ayayayaaa!" Rowana yelled, unencumbered by mental limitations and empowered by the rise and fall of the dangerous electricity coursing through her body.

The spirit of the wolf howled back, deep and profound, as if ecstatic to have found its matching soul. A raven passed by, picking up her immaterial message to deliver to her ancestors and family now decimated by a wave of human evolution they could neither understand nor adapt to. She was the only material proof left of a tier of knowledge in humanity's history who knew how to understand Nature, how to thank Her for the nurturing offered in return, and how to connect with the realm of the spirits. Over the last century, her ancestors had migrated north into Canada from the mid-west, pushed by the scorching weather that had depleted the land of its fecundity. It took her a while to readjust to the new surroundings. It was only after identifying the patch of forest that would become her ceremonial ground that her soul would find a level of peace.

Rowana let the rattle fall, and her hands touched the grass. She pushed her fingers into the mushy soil, reconnecting with the underground world. The heavy scent of the layers of composting pine needles, moss, and twigs almost choked her. With eyes closed but mind alert, she pushed her thoughts beyond the clearing to those waiting for the sign that she was the same loving, empathic, energy-sensitive being representing their tribe in the same way a time capsule might.

Trauma, pain, and injustice poured through the shivering, emptying her and releasing the hooks that might have kept her in a state of spiritual stagnation. The intensity of her chanting increased, allowing energy to download and fill her almost pristine shell.

The ancestors were there for her like a shield against the ever-pervasive dominating and consuming civilization. No one else wanted the knowledge she accumulated during these ceremonial sessions: how to reach and awaken the inner self, how to live nimbly on the exhausted land, and why one should acknowledge a part of the energy matrix that touched everyone. The members of her computerized society wanted access to every material need while their minds were permanently connected to the crystal cloud, conversing in virtual chatrooms.

The pandemics ravaging the world every three years with reinforced strains, the twisted weather escalating dangerously, and the blanket of electromagnetic waves triggered significant alterations within the human body, weakening the molecular structure of its water. People's skins withered, internal organs failed, and the population was diminished.

Rowana had witnessed people who were blackmailed by immoral governments to get the crystal implant in return for their daily necessities. The tiny amorphous device helped download the latest version of the operating system already woven into their psychosomatic networks.

No reassurance of any medical doctor or government official could convince her to adopt the enhancement, altering her pristine, God-given body with such insane built-in intelligence.

She didn't want to go back to that spiritually dry world where people noticed and admired her elongated pitch-black eyes and hair reaching down to her waist. They marvelled at her unadulterated Indigenous features, disregarding the ancient wisdom to which she repeatedly implored them to listen. She felt uprooted even if she had been born in a suburb of the metropolis and had access to the same gadgets that made life complacent. Her colleagues' faces—masks of permanent rictuses—made her feel even more displaced, pushing her to find the solace of the natural cathedral each time an anxiety attack hit her.

She wanted to stitch herself into the canvas of the ground, already decorated with pastels of greens, reds, and browns, held in place by the roots of the oaks, and become one with them, offering her bark to her ancestors to draw upon the untold story of their disappearance, but the message she received was one of relentlessness. She would try one more time to transform those from the city. After that, she would definitely put down roots in the forest.

The city expelled her. It didn't like what she represented: the vestige of a world that had to be destroyed so a newer, more evolved one could take its place. She felt like a bad seed in danger of soiling the healthy ones while waiting to be sown.

The system pushed her out and deleted her digital imprint from all databases requiring identification in return for her daily social needs.

This forest patch had become her home for the two seasons, dry and rainy, equally splitting the year. Society's shunning gave her the respite for her deeper inner inquiry and the answers that seemed to escape her rational mind in the tumultuous city life.

Her soul screamed for recognition from behind her daily mask, painted with grimaces, smiles, euphoria, or clouds of unhappy memories. It was Love that her soul wanted to share with the world. Its restlessness would soon break the Teutonic armour whose pristine voice and childish manifestation had been oppressed by society for centuries. God never gave up on a soul.

Once awoken into the bliss of the ever-present Divinity, the soul started a quest that would never be quenched by normality, repetition, or dogma-altered minds over the dark millennia. The Soul becomes a spiritual Don Quixote, venturing into uncharted territories of feelings, sensations, and enhanced experiences, yearning for a deeper reconnection with its Father that was lost at birth.

Rowana missed the company of other humans. The hut she had built at the edge of the clearing where she held her invocation ceremonies had taken almost half of the dry season to build. In her tempestuous departure from the jungle of the city, a survival kit was the last thing in her mind. A rusty, almost blunt machete was her only cutting tool against the stubborn, twisted vines and supple branches that went into the making of the one-room structure in which she lived.

She had built it on stilts to avoid the occasional flooding during rainy seasons and the annoying rodents that seemed to gain agility and ferocity along with virus variants haunting the world. She'd turned discarded wooden railway beams gathered from a now deserted station at the edge of the city into a solid floor. Petroleum leaks from cars that had carried the precious commodity for decades gave the wood a heavy smell, inducing restless nights, and sometimes, headaches. Even with heavier cutting equipment at her disposal, Rowana wouldn't have had the heart to cut down the healthy, proud Douglas firs for no reason other than to increase her own safety, especially when the forest was already giving her enough protection and nourishment: the occasional hare caught in a primitive trap, mushrooms, and a bounty of wild berries.

While building her sanctuary, to break the monotony of the physical work, she started a diary. Excitement at the thought of keeping her mind busy writing elevated her motivation to push forward and maintain her inner energy at a level of vibration that would allow her to connect to the ancestors' spirits at will. She knew they supported her decision of the permanent break from the city. There was nothing else for her to learn and no one to teach it in the technological matrix.

Over time, plastic bags, pieces of cracked, muddied tarp, empty bottles, and other junked objects littering the forest floor were put to good use. In jars of different colours and sizes, she grew seedlings of lettuce, cabbage, onion, and some nightshades like tomatoes and peppers. When the heavy rain and unceasing winds hit, the safety of the forest clearing would cover the patch of ground she called a "greenhouse," even if the battered tarp that formed the roof were released from the clutches of craggy roots.

After five months of keeping a diary, Rowana noticed the last row of every entry was "I miss seeing other human beings." She loved the company of her wild, furry friends, the whisper of the evergreens, and the sensation of touching the plush moss covering the stones embedded in the forest floor. To compensate for her lack of human interaction, she talked out loud to the physical and invisible worlds, not expecting an answer.

She was aware of the slim chance that a man or woman would wander near or stumble onto her abode. The sweet trap of accepting technology-assisted evolution provided city dwellers with the amenities to live a shallow life while keeping them in a state of permanent surveillance. Escaping that thick layer of complacency and safety required the determination of a cockroach who'd had the luck of stubbornly surviving consecutive extermination raids.

Somehow, the omnipresent security sieve had unaccounted-for holes. It was the middle of the rainy season when the first woman took shape on the other side of the clearing as a clothed ghost. Squalid clouds hung near the tips of the trees, pounding the ground with dense precipitation.

Rowana noticed the newcomer's step hesitate mid-air when spotting the hut. She waved at her, hoping her friendly gesture would not be distorted by the curtain of fluid. "It is safe here," she wanted to shout, but only a whisper fluttered across her lips, as she was unsure if the hunched silhouette wasn't another mirage.

The woman came closer, appearing to struggle through the wet, tall grass, clutching at her ankles. Under the makeshift awning, Rowana moved backward to make space for the woman.

'I'm Roxana,' the petite brunette said, still hugging herself in the dark-brown waterproof raincoat that hung on her like a sack. Every feature on her face was a miniature. Timid fractal patterns embossed the unevenness of the skin around her eyes. They could be of the same age, Rowana thought, immediately loving the rhyming of their names.

Without thinking, she stormed over to embrace the drenched, trembling being. It felt like welcoming home a lost child. Rowana almost had to kneel to get to her eye level; then she introduced herself.

There was not much talking that evening as the newcomer adjusted to the new surroundings on her own terms. She smiled warmly when offered dry clothes, though they were several sizes too large. They shared food and then the bed, lying side by side on the stained, double-size mattress Rowana had saved from the dump and washed in a nearby stream. Her body stiffened, intuitively preventing her from hugging Roxana again out of pure joy that she was no longer alone after such a long time. She breathed slowly, controlling her internal emotions, but she couldn't contain the happy tears when Roxana's tiny hand rested on her chest like a child looking for the reassurance of her mother.

The ancestors' spirits had answered her plea for another soul. Days after Roxana's arrival, Rowana prepared for a ceremony to thank those protecting her from beyond the thin veil separating the realms.

She also needed an apprentice.

Step by step, with the calmness and wisdom of a sage, Rowana described the responsibility she had as the last surviving member of her tribe: "Every time we pay our respects and gratitude to Mother Nature, every time we invoke the spirits of the forest and of the water, we restore some balance to the world."

Rowana broke the flow of movement while arranging the sacramental items on the frail rug and locked her sight on Roxana's. "The ancestors made me aware of other tribes surviving out there. They are spread thin, far and wide. We have to start rebuilding the energetic mesh around the Earth." She touched the tobacco leather pouch gently before continuing. "People like you, escaping from the technological matrix to join us, is what we need to strengthen the power of our invocations and speed the Earth's healing. I'll teach you everything I know as we live by our customs."

And a teacher she became for the former city dweller, opening up an entire universe of possibilities in Nature for Roxana.

Within weeks, love had sewn them together into a tiny Amazonian unit determined to endure the trying times. Theirs was the love of a mother and daughter, even if the age difference was almost insignificant. Their physical size had determined that relationship almost from the beginning, as Rowana assumed the responsibility of protecting Roxana for the purpose of caring for her and transferring her knowledge.

At the seam between the seasons, a young couple pushed through the thickness of the forest. Their bodies bony, their clothing in tatters. They walked straight, each of them carrying a backpack. It wasn't raining, so there was nothing to distort the reality in front of Rowana's eyes. She waved her hand in a motherly welcoming gesture.

Over warm soup, Joanna and Paul shared their story, or bits of it—the less painful parts, as Rowana was led to believe based on the furtive exchange of their gaze. They were married and childless. In the society they were from, he was a mechanical engineer, and she was a hairdresser. Now and then, the young woman touched her belly as if casting a potent spell that might ignite her fertility. *Maybe the ancestors will help her, too,* Rowana thought. *Children bring hope to a community and news from the spirit world as well.*

Together, they selected a spot for a new hut and made plans to enlarge the greenhouse and bring water closer to them by storing it in the large canisters Rowana had not found a use for until then. There was no other direction but forward, moving with the flow of Nature as they helped enrich each other's lives.

(First published in the anthology Moving Forward by Immigrant Writers Association - 2021)

Chapter 4

Knowledge Keepers

I became aware of myself when I turned three. I didn't know the concept of age, but my mother made concerted efforts, through persuasive repetition, to make me repeat this magic number that seemed to make her happy when I answered correctly.

I remember bathtime and my first reflection in the mirror, translucent whiteskin exposed here and there, sinuous lines of dark colour on my legs and hands.

"Mommy, who painted under my skin?" I asked innocently.

She giggled while clenching the sponge, wet with water and soap. "Those are veins through which blood flows. That's what keeps you moving. Look," she said, and she twisted her naked arms up so I could see the crook of her elbow where the veins created patterns similar to the ones on my body.

"Who put them there?" I asked.

She continued to rub my skin gently as if removing an invisible and persistent layer of dirt. "The Creator. We are of Divine origin."

"How do you know?"

She stopped her movement on my skin and fixed me in her turquoise eyes through the blonde hair escaping from her bun.

I always wondered why Mom's patience during bath-time increased tenfold. She moved the sponge in slow strokes, from beneath my chin to my belly, then up my side, up and down my arms, and then on my back. My legs were always last. She was never in a hurry. It was as if she were studying me, looking for physical changes that might alarm any mother.

Though a soothing atmosphere engulfed me every time she initiated the routine, there was a restlessness inside me, and I wanted the weekly activity to end quickly. There were wooden animals and heroes sculpted by my father waiting for me to engage them in the games my mind would create anew, but my eagerness subsided, melting away as I fell under my mother's spell. I remained docile under her touch, memorizing the map she drew on my body.

Somehow, my head didn't require the same attention. A quick wash and rinse sufficed. I noticed discrimination in the way the different parts of my body were treated when I turned five. By then, counting was second nature, and my memory was sharper.

"How are we of Divine origin, Mommy?"

She never answered this question. We were in the kitchen at the time. She was peeling potatoes for a stew while I drew the ocean, the whales, and the fish with colouring pens on pieces of paper my father had received in payment for the day's catch of fish. The flow of Mom's right hand, the one holding the knife, didn't falter. She'd expected me to bring up the subject that was barely discussed between us.

"Previous generations were marked by Divinity in a way that will be revealed to you soon, never skipping a generation, never following a gender pattern. It is written the ancestors watch over each newborn, assess his or her strengths, character, and decision-making abilities, then infuse the body's energy with a Divine stamp.

"We should see such signs in you soon," Mom said without raising her eyes to check my reaction.

The unrelenting investigation of my body, I thought. An immediate current coursed through me, confirming my assumption. *Would Mom show me her marks of Divine origin? Or Dad?* I didn't dare ask, afraid of rejection.

"Your father was not an only child but the youngest of three. One of his sisters has the signs, and I have them, too," Mom added after a longer pause.

My whales were happy in the water. Waves smashed against their raised dorsal fins.

"You will turn six in four months. I'll stop reading your thoughts then."

"Why?" I asked.

"You'll be considered a mature individual by our customs then. The appearance of the Divine on your skin confers you total privacy when it comes to what you think. Memories will surface."

"Memories?"

"We are reborn with memories. And it is our duty as keepers of wisdom and knowledge to share it within the community."

"Everything we remember?" I asked, not realizing the weight of the responsibility I would have if chosen.

"Written records are elusive and frail. Water, fire, or mould could devour a whole library if neglect settles in. Our race has lost so many valuable teachings, technologies, poems, and hymns when we placed our trust in perishable mediums. The small number of volumes in our possession are kept to remind us of the skills and creativity we have."

She dropped the chicken breast, cut into small cubes by her precise moves, into the water boiling in the pot.

"Maybe the scribes pleaded with the Creator to spare their work," I said, colouring the sun and dotting the sky with flocks of birds, tiny broken lines in a V-shaped arrangement.

"Maybe," Mom agreed.

"I like my drawings to be different according to whether I am sad or joyful. I choose the colours to match my mood. I think the scribes got tired of copying the same books over and over and requested a favour from the Creator."

Mom chuckled. Her palms were red from the effort of peeling and cutting and washing the pots. She sat in front of me at the table and reached for my hands. I felt her warmth transferring to me like a mukuna vine wrapping around the tree that would become its home.

Mom went along with my speculation. "I am glad their request was heard and acted upon. It's safer for our history to be written on our skin and shared by many of us at the same time."

I nodded, sadness pushing down on my shoulders as I thought that the ancient rules would soon prohibit Mom from knowing my needs.

* * *

"Mom...Mom." I flew down the stairs, two steps at a time, cheeks burning and heart pumping hard to sustain my excitement. "Mom, look!" I knew I'd find her in the kitchen where family magic happened through her never-resting hands. She was the first to enter that space full of enigmatic combinations of ingredients and love and the last one to leave it after each item used in the cooking process had been washed and put back in its place.

"I got a mark on my right thigh. Look!" I raised the edge of my short pants to expose a dark, embossed, jagged contour and ran my finger over the soft bump. "What is it?"

Mom wiped her hands on a worn piece of cloth taken from the countertop and came closer. She squeezed her eyes and touched the sign, moving her finger along the line as if trying to extract her own memories. "This is your first, so I am allowed an interpretation. The next ones are for you to decipher."

I nodded.

"Danubia is the name of the territory. Millennia ago, our ancestors originated there. There is no memory beyond that point in time. There is memory of the first settlements, the first domesticated animals, and the creation of rituals."

"Is that knowledge embedded in the sign?" I asked.

"Yes, it's all there. You have to focus and wait with patience. These stories will be told around the campfire in the summer and at the community gatherings after the harvests have been secured and the snow outside tells us that another cycle has ended."

I sat at the short end of the kitchen table, looking at my mother but not really seeing her, eyes fixed on an invisible point in the horizon. "How many signs will I get?"

"None of us knows in advance. I think it depends on how much history each of them contains. Some of us have poured these stories out for many years, using only one or two signs. The history might go deep. Details count. Relationships and alliances are worth mentioning. The scale of time is important," she said.

"Was this story told by others before? How do you know about it?"

She cracked a smile, her eyes in tears. "I remember having this sign in a previous life, but ..."

I waited patiently.

"But I feel yours goes deeper into the daily customs of the Danubians, their personal dramas and celebrations, the wars and much more."

She was not done. I kept looking at the horizon.

"Some stories repeat at certain intervals when the Divine thinks the new generations might forget them or that there are not enough elders to share them."

Mom walked away to check the pie in the oven, but I could still see the smile that had moved the corner of her mouth. Maybe she knew that the imprint on my skin was the beginning of a century-old saga that I would still be telling in my old age.

* * *

The shadows lingered on the book making reading difficult. I was too lazy to crawl toward the remaining sunny spot on the bed. The volume grew heavy in my hands as if the paper had suddenly thickened, trying my strength.

Black leather embossed with cursive silvery writing—the Book of Rituals.

I knew all the steps of initiation by heart and even anticipated some of the questions I might be asked by the twelve children, ages six to eight, waiting for me outside. I was about to end the preparations for my fourth ceremony, and each time, the curiosity of the little ones bubbled up in similar inquiries.

The physical book represented an anchor to the past, a

reminder that knowledge could still be preserved that way in certain circumstances. I pushed myself up off the wooden bed, putting aside the woollen blanket hanging on the edge. My attention shifted to the bare walls, coloured charcoal due to generations of candle smoke settling on the wood, forming a protective layer. The outside light didn't enter, keeping the main room in a permanent state of semi-obscurity. This was the cottage of the initiators in which many thousands before me mentally prepared for ceremonies.

There were no paintings, no insignias, and no distracting objects, just one empowering carving above the entrance: *When helping a brother, keep your mind void of expectations and your heart filled with love*; a motivating message indeed, one that had been entrenched in our psyches since childhood.

The coolness of the floorboards sent a shiver through my entire body. *I need some motivation*, I thought, and I drew on the energy I'd just invoked, my right hand tracing the contours of the signs on my opposite arm and shoulder and my legs and the chest. The energy was there, arising from the stories, poems, and experiences of the past generations, and a soothing vibration reoriented my attention and charged every cell.

I closed my eyes to centre myself before standing up. I knew I might get dizzy if I didn't give the energy enough time to dissipate through my body. Outside, the noise of childhood interaction grew louder. I put on a sweater, tidied my hair with my fingers, and shoved a hat on my head.

Two sips of water from the blue glass bottle on the table reflecting the rays of the sun soothed my parched throat. I opened the cabin door and stepped outside on the porch.

The chatter froze, and the children all looked in my direction. Then, like well-trained cadets, they shuffled to the bench reserved for their age group. Most of the six-year-olds had recently received their first signs, but the introverts were always harder to interact with. They needed special attention and a telepathic approach when it came to piquing their interests and gaining their trust.

My bare feet welcomed the softness of the soil. The children were all barefoot, as well. It was our way of maintaining an energetic umbilical cord to the Earth and one of the first lessons we learned in school.

Towering pines defined the clearing, which was large enough to hold several cottages. Straight paths spread toward the nearby lake, the meditation patch, the herb garden, and the healing wheel. Stones and crystals were placed on the ground in a large circle. The benches formed a U-shape in front of the initiators' cottage.

I walked toward the children to a spot where the sunlight would still rest on my shoulders.

When camp was nearly over, it was time for questions and answers, an unrestrained chat that blurred the line between teacher and pupil, and the children knew they could ask me anything...within reason.

"How many signs have you been blessed with?" asked a blond boy sitting on the bench with the other six-year-olds.

I took a step closer, leaned forward, and whispered, "George, you know that question is on the forbidden list—are you trying to trick me?" I continued, my voice raised: "The number is not important; the meaning is."

"When did they stop appearing for you?" George asked a pertinent question this time.

"Two years ago, when I turned fourteen. Somehow, I knew the large dragon on my back would complete the imprints."

"A dragon!" everyone murmured in admiration.

"Is it true that signs might disappear after the whole story had been told?" an eight-year-old asked once the commotion had subsided.

"Yes, that's true. If the story is exhausted, and the community has learned from it and has an imprint of the experiences, the mark will be gone."

I walked to a spot where I could face all three benches. "Cases when a sign is replaced with a new one are rare. Maybe, in extreme situations, when messages have to be delivered for the survival of the community."

They were engaged again as every detail would enhance the acuity of their reading of the signs.

"Would you tell us the story of the dragon?" several of them pleaded.

I breathed in the fragrant air, infused with the smell of moss, pine, and moist leaves sent by the gentle wind from the east. A baby storm was brewing.

We should be packed and gone by the time the wet weather reaches this spot, I thought.

"This is a really long story. It stretches multiple generations—"

"Of dragons?"

"Of dragons and humans," I said. "This is the third consecutive life in which I've been chosen to tell the drag-ons' stories."

"You were reborn with so many memories," Tania, an eight-year-old girl, tiny as a squirrel, said admiringly.

"Indeed, but I shared with other communities in my previous lives."

Bodies leaned forward, their mouths rounded in awe. There was no escape. The web of magic they anticipated had to be unravelled with enough impact for the memories to last not only this lifetime, but if triggered properly, ignited in successive ones. I sat on a stump on the invisible line that would make the U-shape of benches into a square.

"Dragons are not to be feared but embraced for their purity, energy, and dedication to the highest purpose."

None of them tried to interrupt with a bad joke or even a question. I had caught them all unintentionally in my net. I felt like a lucky fisherman.

"They are beautiful creatures, invisible to us when we don't make the effort to raise our own vibrations. These are the skills we learn in school. Yes, we are the chosen ones, for the signs manifest through us and make us special, but if we apply the techniques deeply, we go to the next highest level."

I pushed the soles of my feet down on the forest soil. My own energetic umbilical cord felt strong and reassuring. I started with the basics. "Dragons live in the ninth dimension and higher," I said. "I mean the really old ones that are thousands of years old."

I wanted to stand up and walk, propelled by the excitement I always felt when talking about the subject, but I stayed put. "There are 'gofer' dragons, as well, not to diminish their qualities and importance. They whirl between different dimensions with orders, sanctions, and energetic downloads for those requiring spiritual attention, a correctional nudge, or a life-changing lesson."

"My mom told me they are bearers of light who carry the divine blueprint," Tania interjected when I paused to gather my thoughts.

I nodded.

Everyone's head raised in the direction of far-distant thunder.

"Enough about dragons for now. Let's recap what we've learned in the last three days," I said, looking for my first target. I picked an eight-year-old with freckles running wild on his cheeks.

"How do you bring out the whole story of a sign?" The boy leaned forward, elbows on his knees, and without buying any time, said, "Feeling its contour is important, but the journey starts way before that internally." He stopped, looking for confirmation.

"Continue," I said.

"Our elders always encourage us to ask for help from our invisible guides. They give us strength and an inner ability to see what our eyes can't perceive."

"Very well. We must remember that we are not alone on this wonderful journey," I said, knowing they'd heard it many times before.

I drew a line in the soil with my toe and chose another question. "What is the physical manifestation indicating one has been chosen to share his or her stories with another community?" It was a contentious subject. Even if honourable by ancient standards, leaving one's friends and family behind ignited sadness in the selected souls.

I pointed to Sona this time, a seven-year-old girl with short brown hair and bright eyes set deep into the caverns of the eye sockets. "The acknowledgement is a process that might take up to four weeks," she said. "Owls of different colours crowd nearby in a spectacle of hoots and cries, setting the place for the hawks and lastly, for the ravens. It's a succession of birds that can't be mistaken for anything else. Their gurgling croaks turn into harsh grating sounds enough to drive the chosen one's family crazy." Her voice was much livelier than her gloomy presence."

"Sona is right. Are there any other phenomena that could indicate such selection?" I asked. I knew what I referred to was encountered much less frequently, but in my opinion, it was more powerful.

"A body of water could spring out of the ground near the house," Sona said, more asking than confirming.

I was delighted, so I pushed for more: "What's next after such manifestations are acknowledged?"

"The family must hang a quilt representing some of the signs carried by its members over the years. It's a gesture of acceptance. Only then will the birds' visits cease."

"And the preparation for the trip begins," I said. "There is sadness with such a loss, but I want you to consistently remind yourself that when spread, these stories will be enjoyed by many who survive in distant lands."

A hand shot up. It was Tania again. I nodded.

"But after our return home, could they distort the stories without us there as a permanent check on their accuracy?"

"Tania, sometimes our stories make a full circle and reach us here.

"Yes, they are changed by people's imaginations, the desire to please, or even with a pretense of ownership, and we shouldn't mind. Our stories give purpose by creating imaginary quilts in those listening to them."

I moved my feet, levelling the soil to create a new drawing board to illustrate what I would say next. "Imagine those who go through multiple lives without remembering any of them—how lucky are we by comparison?"

The thunder shook the ground again, telling us to pack up and go. "Meet everyone back here when you hear my whistle. Let's move out before the pouring starts."

I did not move. Thunder roiled. Lightning cracked the slowly darkening sky, coming closer and closer, prodding the forest for the best place to discharge. The energy coursed through my feet, reassuring me not to be afraid—I'd be spared as I had not yet finished telling my stories.

* * *

"How did it go?"

I was back from the camp. Mother and I were in the kitchen, facing each other over the table's worn wooden top. I quietly sipped a glass of cold-pressed vegetable juice made from her favourites: kale, celery, and carrots. Patties of the leftover fibre mixed with eggs, salt, pepper, and turmeric fried in the pan. The slightly open window faced the backyard and let in a gentle breeze, diluting the dense vapours above the stove.

"Everyone is prepared. They are excited to be the chosen ones, to have a purpose," I said.

"You were the same," Mother said, her gestures calm as she set down her mug.

I wanted her to read my thoughts again like she did before I'd turned six. I craved the intimacy of the silent, effortless communication that had put me internally at ease, but that was no longer possible—I was an adult, teaching others about life's phases of storytelling.

"The times are changing, Mom," I said, not totally sure the thought I'd expressed was my own. "These children want more than just to hear and retell stories from an ancient past. I've accepted that I am just a bearer of a divine message that no longer belongs to me once I've released it into the world, but—"

"Non-attachment is embedded in our DNA," Mom interjected as if trying to end my emotional struggle."

"Maybe their DNA is changing." Saying it out loud scared me. The daring words cut through millennia of customs, somehow diminishing the sacrifice of previous generations.

Mom picked up the mug and tilted it a bit, pretending, avoiding my gaze. Over time, I learned to recognize the gesture indicating she had no words.

"They feel responsible for the accuracy of the stories long after it ceases to be their duty to maintain it. They are willing to accept slight alterations but not distortions."

"What are you saying?" Mom asked.

"These might be the generations that will never come back to us. Our numbers will dwindle, our own existence..."

I couldn't finish the damning sentence.

Mom's hands grabbed the edge of the table till her knuckles went white. "What happens when they reach maturity?"

I had considered that scenario myself on the way back from the camp after reflecting on the children's perception of their deeper obligation. "Some might come back to give birth here, some will not. The strong-willed will not marry outside the community, keeping the customs intact, even if travelling to faraway lands. For others, love will be stronger than the blood calling." My heart sank, heavy with the perspective of doom.

"How is this DNA mutation good for our people?" Mom said, staring at the empty mug.

"I don't know, Mom. Maybe the Divine has a plan we need to follow. Maybe this is the price we must pay for who we are.

"I will keep the faith and carry on with my stories." Sharing the stories of Danubia and of the dragons was my life's purpose. I would marry soon and have children who, once they had gone into the world, might forget the path back to the spiritual hive. I could only pray that would never happen to our family.

"Selfish or not, I am glad this...genetic mutation, as you call it, didn't occur until now," Mom said, a faint smile breaking her serious composure.

I leaned over, covered her hands with mine, and sent her a reassuring thought: "I, too, am glad, Mom."

(First published in the anthology Reborn With Memories by Immigrant Writers Association - 2023)

Chapter 5

Water Confessions

This stand-alone chapter is part of Volume 3 of the *Water* book series, following *Water Entanglement* (vol 1) and *Crystal Cloud* (vol 2). While the series offers a richer experience when read in order, the following key details will help the reader fully enjoy this chapter on its own.

• Society has changed due to increased climate turbulence generated by the Sun's hyperactivity.

• Some places are covered by domes in order to shield them from the harsh weather.

• A crystal-based technology was developed for human use. The crystal is embedded in the eye's cornea and connected to the pineal gland through nanobots. When drops of structured water (water whose molecular structure is in the shape of a hexagon) come in contact with the crystal, the memory of water gets decoded, and healing in the human body takes place.

Cherry moved to Hawaii, to Marinka's home, months after she'd willingly accepted the shungite crystal implants.

It brought her an inner peace that only her daydreaming could provide in the past when she'd sparingly indulged.

Cherry followed her daily post-breakfast ritual: outside on the lawn barefoot, wearing shorts and a skimpy top and holding a cup of chai tea. With her left hand, she whipped into shape the fallen blue-striped cushion on the wooden chair, then sat down.

The entire plot of land on which both houses were built, Marinka's and her father's, was enclosed by an aluminum composite, tinted, covered dome, allowing transparency from the inside out and letting in only a certain amount of UV rays. Gone were the days when she sipped from the tea, eyes closed, her body twisted slightly toward the east as she fully inhaled the ionized air, feeling the salty taste going down her throat like life's current. She would then turn toward the west, where the richly-blossomed plumeria were planted, and inhaled again. No scent tingled her nostrils this time.

Kahuna used to take care of the plants, Marinka had told her a few weeks after the elder's passing in 2060. He had mingled together the different fragrances—sweet, spicy, jasmine, citrus, and even orange—as if he wanted to keep the flowers in a permanent state of wonder as to which strain of plumeria they belonged. Now, hosted under the dome, only the ghosts of those natural marvels survived in the selective light spectrum.

She waved at the Laysan albatross perched on the edge of the cliff, knowing they would not see her and react to her gesture. The birds kept a precarious balance against the wind, a tad stronger than usual. It ruffled their feathers and hopped about in small bursts, bumping into each other as they competed for space. After a while, even the flyers understood that the ocean below, devoid of life, would no longer provide the once plentiful food: fish, crabs, mussels, clams, or the rare, washed-out body of a baby dolphin. Before the dome was put in place, the albatross had fought for the scraps Cherry had thrown at them once a day or over Hawaiian petrel eggs in burrows or rock crevices, but that food had also grown scarce.

Behavioural changes in animals and birds were no longer subtle, and over the past twenty years since she'd arrived on the island, Cherry had been in a perfect position to witness most of them.

Somehow, her once alabaster skin had borrowed a lighter nuance from Marinka's Indigenous colour, as if the island was working hard to turn her into a Native, too.

Cherry didn't need sunglasses. The thin shungite crystal layer[1] over her cornea reflected the light, retaining only a fraction of it for power while maintaining its connection with the crystal cloud that hovered invisibly above them at fifteen thousand feet. Over the years, the shungite mesh had encircled the earth, facilitating faster and more secure communication for the billion or so people locked into the geographic locations deemed safe from the damaging weather and increased radiation.

The International Aeronautics and Space Agency, formerly known as NASA, had selected that October day in 2078 for the launch of the final shuttle to the Metamorphosis orbital station, a staging place before the start of the never-to-return intergalactic trip to Enceladus, one of Saturn's moons.

Now, the Agency was in the hands of the USA's largest debtors—China, Japan, and Russia—to settle their financial debt. Due to the political and economic turmoil of the late 2020s, the balance of power had shifted toward the BRICS nations[2] and stayed there against all odds, in spite of the Western country's efforts to prevent it from happening.

Cherry cared little about politics. Even the global economy didn't mean much to her. She only focused on local matters these days: the daily farmer's market, the guitar quartet playing at The Realm on Thursday nights, and the monthly art shows dotting the boardwalk on the weekend.

She sniffed at the air again, knowing the highly efficient air filtration system would not make any exceptions for her. Ojani, her long-time friend, was on that shuttle. He was the only one she still kept in contact with from Toronto, aside from Ilanda, while she was alive. Cherry leaned deeper into the chair as if anchoring herself, then, with her eyes closed, she mentally connected to the crystal cloud. Her unique digital signature stormed through the maze of the ether and identified itself in front of several proxies and DMZs[3] until it reached the virtual chatroom created for those to say their goodbyes.

A crease on her forehead intensified her focus as she sent a *handshake* signal to Ojani.

The man, with his unceasing smile and orangey skin, appeared in her mind's eye. He was wearing the Jamaican, happy shirt that had always infused colour and laughter in the Toronto lab. It was also why Ilanda, the renowned neurosurgeon and the developer of crystal technology, had attached herself to him. She needed his energy, love, and respect.

"Ready to take off?" Cherry asked, smiling back at him

from the lawn in Hawaii. "You still haven't given them a reason to kick you out?"

"In fact, we are still debating over the number of tropical shirts I can bring with me and the time allotted for wearing them on the intergalactic trip, eh? Too much happiness and too many good times could be dangerous, eh?" he said. He showed his white teeth in a large grin surrounded by his now silvery beard.

"It could be a deal-breaker, indeed," she played along. "How do you feel?"

Each time they connected that way, she asked him questions and pried into his emotional state. She managed her approach like a doctor placing one acupuncture needle after another, waiting for a reaction from the patient's body. A finer muscle spasm would tell her where the next needle should go in order to release some of the pressure required for effective healing.

"Physically, I am border-lining the bottom edge, but as you know, my generous funding for this project and the health waiver I signed when I decided to fly out make my personal stats irrelevant. They don't care if I die before we reach the Metamorphosis docking station."

Ojani shrugged and waved his hand as if he had just said something banal and not worthy of Cherry's attention, but then he shrugged and continued: "I really feel out of place, like an old tree, dry and hollow, its arteries clogged, begging for a drop of sap."

Cherry felt the tickling of tears coursing down her cheeks.

"I never knew Jamaica, the country of my parents and ancestors, intimately. I was only told about the happy times and positive vibes exuded by the land. Lamenting doesn't do me any good, eh, now that I am almost uprooted for the second time, but this time, it's my choice." He paused for a moment, looking off-camera.

"An old tree looking for new soil," Cherry said, filling the silence.

"I doubt I'll reach the destination," Ojani said. "Planting new shoots from the ashes of this body will be a riff of awe. I live with the consolation that I can offer support to the generations born on this lengthy, one-way trip to the unknown.

"What about you, eh?" he asked, shrugging off the tightness in his voice. "Who will celebrate your birthday with you? It's coming up in two weeks, eh?"

Cherry smiled. She had the impression she'd blushed at the reminder. "Seventy-two years on this amazing planet that has suffered irreversible changes," she said. *What an accomplishment to reach 2078 almost unscathed, Cherry thought. I'll turn seventy-two years young in two weeks. Not only did I survive the turmoil of 2055 when the explosion at the Water for All conference in Toronto changed my life by unwittingly triggering the awakening of water, but I lived to see how, several years later, the network of crystal clouds helped the disintegration of secular governments subservient to the currency masters. I have been so lucky!*

There were not enough years left for her to be present at Earth's next phase as it continued to hold on to the remnants of humanity. She would be gone by the time the tidal wave of destruction manifested in climate change, causing the disturbance of Earth's magnetic poles to cease before taking a deep breath and pushing back in the opposite direction.

Everyone's life mimicked Don Quixote's struggle to tame the stubborn windmill—that is what her father used to say after reading to her from the famous book.

"Marinka will be around. She might throw a surprise party here on the lawn. What better birthday gift than to watch a flaming sunset with a tasty tea in hand?" she said.

"Still manless these days—you, too, eh?" Ojani asked jokingly and winked at her.

"No one worthy enough to attend such a pretentious party," she shot back. "Women only; that's the rule of the house."

They both giggled at their tussle of words.

"Another layer of crystal was added at seventy-five thousand feet as a relay for the one we are using right now, eh?"

She knew the meaning of that, but she let him continue.

"We can chat while on Metamorphosis. They said we'll stay there for one month for physical adaptation before we start the big trip, eh?"

"Yes, that will be nice. During that time, I'll be the thread still linking you to Earth," Cherry reassured, more hot tears running down her cheeks.

A red warning flashed in the virtual chatroom, announcing the end of the session.

"Takeoff is approaching," Ojani said. His hand touched the pixels of her face. "This is the closest I'll be to you for a long, long time, my friend."

Cherry had expected his characteristic "eh" to close his affectionate statement, but the emotion might have suffocated the exclamation.

"Stay safe. I need to hear real news from you, none of

the propaganda. I'll meet you and Ilanda again in the Infinite Consciousness when the time comes," she said. And she'd meant it. Humanity's latest enterprise—the intergalactic trip to Titan—should have pristine ethics, impeccable person-to-person interaction, a low egotistical level, and an increased consciousness.

Would any individual still holding his low vibration make it to the team by using flattering keywords? She hoped not. That unique individual could become the incipient phase of a virus in its atrophied form, waiting for the proper environment to flourish. While in space, the person-virus would leave its petri dish unobserved as in shedding his fake persona.

As a limnologist, Cherry knew how insidious and dangerous an infestation could be. On the space shuttle, the person-virus, like blue-green algae, would stay at the microscopic level and naturally insert itself into the human ecosystem, asking innocent questions, prying for weaknesses, fattening itself up with data as if it had fed on nutrients such as nitrogen and phosphorus. Like the blue-green algae, the person-virus would bloom when the time was ripe, taunting those already identified as victims and who were being studied. The construct of clumps of lies, diversions, and insinuations would be so dense that not even the most skillful limnologist could fix.

"I will. You too, eh?" Ojani said. The smile seemed to dry on his lips as if he were not capable of showing love for life itself. "I won't be here to hold you accountable for the memoir you promised to write," he continued.

"Ah, that's a job as big as flying to another planet," Cherry said, thinking she would be let off the hook.

He stared at her, the reddish light from the virtual chatroom dimming his features.

"The times you, Ilanda, and I lived in are mulching under the pressure of the recent past and the tumultuous now. By the time we reach Enceladus, the crystal technology, cleaning one lake at a time and teaching the masses about increased consciousness might be irrelevant. Young people are not always interested in the past, but when they are, I want them to find your recollection of what really happened, eh?" Ojani said, sadder than she'd ever seen him before.

Was he nostalgic about leaving Earth? Did he miss Ilanda so much that he would attempt to find consolation on other planets? Even Tenzin[4], the Buddhist monk he loved like a brother?

"If you put it that way, my conscience would feel guilty. I'll do it," she agreed. "The crystal backups should provide support starting in 2060, the year we upgraded to that feature. I'll have to dig through my brain for previous years."

"Or you could fill in the gaps with some quality literature. I mean fiction, eh? No one will notice," Onjani said, his face shimmering and glowing like the moon eclipsing the sun.

Cherry squeezed her eyes tighter as if afraid his image would inexplicably escape the virtual chatroom.

"I can only write technical stuff, you know: test the water of a lake or a river, then neatly arrange the results in several columns, including PH, turbidity, conductivity, hardness, alkalinity, dissolved oxygen, and much more. I can interpret the numbers all day long and create an inspiring paper for my fellow limnologists, but it might bore those youngsters you mentioned to death."

"Now, now, don't underestimate your fiction writing skills, eh?" Ojani said as if to pacify the irked tone he likely sensed in her voice. "You're retired. Sorry to remind you about this exciting phase of your life when time is, and at the same time, is not of the essence. Enrol for a writing course first, eh? Get the basic rules of what it takes to add a flicker of flair and metaphor to otherwise mundane, scientifically-backed papers. You'll shake off the disguise of dryness hidden in the numbers and expose the sweetness or words melted into expository, descriptive, or persuasive paragraphs, eh?"

For a moment, Cherry imagined the intensity of the sun testing the endurance of her skin and the dying wind latching on to her shoulder-length hair and letting it all go at the request of a higher force.

"Based on the vocabulary you're using, should I conclude that you are halfway through such a course?"

"No, I just widen my reading interests. When my services are not required, I spend my time in the library. A number of international scholars are still attached to the decaying epoch of printed books, making a sublime case of why such relics should occupy precious space on the shuttle, eh?"

"They were wisely advised on how to use media in their favour." She chuckled, then continued. "It's comforting to know all the generations born into space will still be able to touch and smell a leather-bound book. Producing them is a now-defunct craft."

"Cherry, my friend, I've decided to leave the past behind, but I've asked you not to. Be objective. Don't dwell in sadness; roar with happiness when it's due. Show our flaws. For what is worth, someone, someday, will read it."

He cupped her virtual face in his hands and kissed her forehead. She felt the heat of his lips...or she thought she did. In her mind, the sun was still hitting her body, increasing the heat beneath what little clothing she was wearing.

"When all is done and sealed, come visit me in spirit," Cherry said, not sure for how long she could hold back her tears.

The warning expired, and the virtual chatroom vanished. He didn't have the chance to reassure her he would travel back from Titan in his ethereal form, but Cherry knew he would. He'd had his roots on Earth for many lifetimes, she assumed. Maybe his karma still needed cleansing on a third-dimensional level.

Her awareness slowly returned to her physical surroundings of restless Layson albatross, the pungent scent of plumeria, and the ancient and primal pull of the ocean, carrying the exhilaration of the waves shoreward, heavy with layers of seaweed entangled in the debris of a messy civilization.

She sipped her lukewarm tea, then connected to an online mainstream media channel broadcasting the takeoff from Wenchang on Hainan Island, China, live.

Cherry would say her goodbyes quietly, embracing everyone on board with thoughts of love.

----

[1] In the previous volume, Crystal Cloud members accept shungite crystal implants that enhance the capabilities of their brains and help heal certain diseases. Shungite is a crystal found only in Siberia. It has amazing properties. One of them is the ability to clean water of its impurities.

[2] BRICS is an intergovernmental organization comprised of Brazil, Russia, India, China, South Africa, Iran,

Egypt, Ethiopia, the United Arab Emirates, and 111 other countries. Originally formed to highlight investment opportunities, the grouping evolved into a cohesive geopolitical bloc, with governments meeting annually at formal summits and coordinating multilateral policies since 2009. Bilateral relations among BRICS are conducted mainly on the basis of non-interference, equality, and mutual benefit.

[3] In computer security, a DMZ—or demilitarized zone—is a physical or logical subnetwork containing and exposing an organization's external-facing services to an untrusted, usually larger network, such as the Internet.

[4] In the first two volumes, Tenzin is introduced as a childhood friend who became a monk. Tenzin asked Ojani to join the monastic order multiple times.

(First published in the anthology Old Roots, New Shoots by Immigrant Writers Association - 2024)

Chapter 6

The Reset

The Space Pilgrims disembarked on the planet's northern hemisphere under the mantle of darkness. The land outside the chosen city was arid, flat, and furrowed by ruts carved by the once-mighty rivers that had given the planet its purpose and power. Now, only rivulets of timid water coursed through the ancient veins of hardened mud. Before dawn peaked over the horizon, the visitors' working drones had paved the road to the edge of the city, and the memory alteration compound had been drizzled over every building within city limits.

No one wondered how or when such a magnificent structure had emerged in their vicinity. At least, not until the image would be ingrained in local folklore and passed on in the written record.

The Federation Council, to which the Space Pilgrims reported, suggested the ship be morphed into one of the most beloved architectural icons the people of Earth called *religious sanctuaries*. They were places of weekly refuge for all ages, a terse respite of calmness in their chaotic struggle for survival. The visitors morphed the ship, inconspicuously adorning it with the peoples' preferred religious symbols, turning it into the abode of tranquillity for which their hearts yearned.

The Space Pilgrims—who could easily infiltrate the minds of the locals—could not make sense of the entangled, restless thoughts in the sacred space, meaning there was no clear direction for themselves or society as a whole. The mental decline also resulted from fear induced by the decimation of the population, a consequence of the struggle over scarce resources and the launch of artificially created diseases in their diabolical laboratories.

The Space Pilgrims were deeply pained at seeing the bald patches of land disfigure the surface like the small craters dotting the lifeless planets they had visited eons ago. The abrasive scars gorged over the once-lush landscape, demonstrating a mindless desire for destruction.

Ancient forests had been decimated. Slick, smelly sludge poured into once-proud expanses of water. Species on the planet had gone extinct at an exponential rate, justifying the Space Pilgrims' intervention, as the historically beautiful ecosystem was in peril.

They tapped into Water's memory as she called them through the nodes connecting the multiverse's energy, a desperate hail asking for help with a task she could no longer handle herself.

Millions of years of Earth's history had been exposed to grit, drama, and abuse. It was these remnants of reticence over which the Federation Council mulled. A tacit witness to the debauchery of Earth, Water faithfully recorded the wisdom and nuances of existence that would otherwise be lost.

Water couldn't be harnessed for long, and the Space Pilgrims were surprised at how often Water had fought back. Each time, she'd awoken to throw off the shackles people had put on her, and she made them pay dearly for their transgression. The Earth was burning from within and without. It was a shattered planet, a piece of broken glass that could only be mended by intervening with people's free will.

The three cultures mingled in the rugged city, each of them idolizing the same almighty entity in their own ways. Faith and a day of rest gathered all of them to the sacred space.

The walls muttered the Almighty's new commandments, preaching restraint for clogging Earth's arteries with the grease of hate and useless competition.

Drops of love lingered in the religious sanctuary's shimmering air, trickling on the heads of devotees, who caught them in their open mouths. It was a blessing for the genetically mutated, a throwback to the primary iteration that had taught people how to respect Water, Air, Earth, and life in general. It wasn't their disobedience that had almost mulched Earth, only the inappropriate use of their free will.

Now, charged with the legitimacy of the priests and prophets, the new commandments would spread throughout the land to every pocket of humanity left, cleansing the global consciousness and rooting out weeds of delusion and instant gratification.

The Space Pilgrims announced the mission's success to the Federation Council, and the morphed ship scheduled its departure. The shell of the religious sanctuary remained behind, brandishing the symbols that had both gathered and segregated people.

Before leaving, the Space Pilgrims put Water in charge, a vigilant steward entangled with Earth as an umbilical cord entangles a mother and her unborn child. Once more, she would save the planet from the creatures depending upon her.

Before flying away, the Space Pilgrims embedded one more message in Water's molecular structure along with a specific threshold parameter: "Next time, call us sooner."

Chapter 7

Fibonacci Gamble

A thin layer of clouds spreads over the bluish sky in a convoluted pattern reminiscent of abstract artwork. Watching their lazy passage through the tinted windows of my office on the second floor of the main CERN building makes me yearn to be outdoors on a grassy hill in Allemogne. The weather was to hold steady at twenty-five degrees Celsius¾my kind of weather¾for the next several days, pushing my mind even further toward organizing a potential hiking weekend.

If only it weren't for the darn government officials' pressure to yield concrete results for any of the still-functional projects, life would be quite good.

I tug at my coat's lapels to straighten them.

What used to be a simple request for funding enough to automatically fill the institute's coffers has turned into a bureaucratic nightmare, a five-levels-of-signatures hell before even one Bitcoin¾electronic, invisible currency that, in the end, I sure to bring down the illegitimate worldwide financial structure¾materializes in any bank accounts. My quantum engineers are the best in the world, but they still can't generate money out of thin air.

I move my focus to the layer of glass in front of me to check once more on my navy-blue-and-black-striped suit wrapped around my medium height and stockily built body; a labour of love generated by many hours spent in the gym. My familiar facial features stare back at me: wide nose, high cheekbones, permanently pale skin no matter how much sun exposure I get, brown eyes and hair so thin at the top it says, "I don't know if I should be combed to the left or to the right." No matter how rarefied my hair looks, I won't shave it; no way! I'll hang onto whatever I have left for as long as I can.

Impatient, I check my watch. Tuleya, my Guyana-born assistant, should usher in the heads running the projects on the still-active particle colliders at any moment.

"Radical change," "shifting direction," and "jump into the unforeseeable" were slogans I thought powerful enough to infuse certain energy in my colleagues, whose idea drainage equated the rate of the disappearance of funds.

Darn economic collapse.

I pace to the door and back several times to calm myself down. The year twenty-twenty would be remembered in CERN's history as the one most countries funding the Institute and main experiments running the Large Hadron Collider withdrew their support. This was due to financial exhaustion triggered by the internal struggle of the insurmountable deficit of paying the pensions of retirees. The large picture on the wall with me squished between the presidents of the USA, Germany, and Japan, the only superpowers still willing to fork over Bitcoin for cherry-picked projects, was proof that history would be changed that day.

I take off my jacket, put it on a hanger on the back of the door, and sit. A quick glance at the sky confirms the clouds' patience on their way from here to there as if they have all the time in the world. They have no deadlines or particles to shoot at each other at enormous speeds through mile-long tunnels buried deep underground.

There's a knock on the door, and my gatekeeper lets in the three department heads, all of them off-the-chart brainiacs.

"Hi, Brian," they say in unison and drop themselves into the chairs already lined up in front of my desk, which is made up of a narrow piece of opaque glass stuck to curvy aluminum legs.

I nod in response. Suddenly, my mouth is dry. I taste metal. It's like I've just finished chewing on a lead pipe. The plastic water bottle leaves a wet mark on the glass table when I pick it up to drink. It does nothing to wash away the awful taste in my mouth.

I lean back in my chair and try to maintain a pose feigning calmness. These guys will be hard to sell on my idea. "So, we're down to three colliders standing," I say, trying to start off light, but there is no emphatic reaction from any of the heavy-set men. All three of them are wearing a goatee as if it were a requirement for employment. "They're the ones running the projects the big bosses are still willing to fund. Everything else is less important," I say, continuing my prepared speech.

I look at them, deer frozen in headlights. Maybe they're thinking they will be part of the next wave of layoffs. This is a situation when one doesn't think of the job at hand but of his own survival.

Pathetic!

I take another sip, assessing which of the middle-aged

men to jump on first. I don't like any of them in particular; I'm here to manage, not to make friends. That statement is so lame—all CEOs claim it like a badge of honour.

Bullshit!

"Have you thought of any new angles to bring financial life back to the moribund body that is CERN?" I ask with a smirk on my face, repeating my request from the email I sent to them two weeks ago.

Iurie Ivanciuk, the Ukrainian-born head of SANCTUARY, an ion collider experiment, shuffles his wide ass in the chair, rests his elbows on the armrests, and moves his lips a bit without making any sound as if almost ready to spit out some words. At the last moment, he remembers to check left and right with his colleagues and gets a nod of approval.

They've come prepared for a potential challenge and even chosen their spokesperson. I like the strategy, so I relax a bit, preparing to be awed.

Ivanciuk, an experimental particle physicist, places a piece of paper in front of me, which I pull in closer to inspect. The list is short and involves the teams left taking care of SANCTUARY, ENCLAVE, and SALVATION.

Renaming the old colliders was a condition imposed by the superpower funders. A sign, they thought, of more prosperous times and abundant positive results.

"Interesting," I reply with a smile, giving them the impression that I'm over the moon with their suggestions, that it is an unexpected cash cow forcing the funds to materialize and bring back the hundreds of physicists, electrical and quantum engineers, software geniuses, and others who had parted with CERN in the last four years.

I stare at the list a moment longer, not reading the words. My mind is already set on the next project to put us in the black. Nevertheless, I want to give them the impression that I appreciate their effort in compiling a list of potential winners.

"Correct me if I'm wrong, but none of these so-called new projects are new. They are, more or less, offshoots of existing ones."

They look at each other, seemingly panicked. All of them shuffle in their seats now, perspiration crowning their high foreheads.

"No need for all of you to talk at the same time," I say. Why use sarcasm at a time like this? I really don't know. Maybe it's to compensate for my own misery at being the youngest CEO in CERN's history because no one from the old guard wanted the title.

"Huh...you're right, but most of the researchers who might have come up with something groundbreaking have left," Matthew Chubuian, the head of ENCLAVE, a general-purpose detector, says, his voice tinged with a whisker of hope. "We still have competent teams, but ..." He leaves the words hanging, not wanting to dig himself deeper into the empty explanation. His receding hairline is gathered in a short ponytail. Overgrown sideburns seem to reach desperately out to his similarly unkempt goatee. Today, his spotted shirt is more crumpled than the light orange one he wore last week. Signs of desperation are plastered all over him.

I place the piece of paper they gave me gently on the desk, then I open the wheeled drawer on my left and pull out three copies of *Seeds for Another Universe* by Mircea Dacian, a Romanian scientist with a list of accomplishments as long as two or three reputable CERN engineers are tall.

The phrase, "Small country, great minds," runs through the winding maze of my thoughts.

"This is a book I want you to read ASAP," I say and push a copy in front of each of them.

"In the nineties, this guy and his team were doing cutting-edge research in a mostly communist country—can you image the conditions they were working in and how imaginative and innovative they had to be in order to overcome their lack of equipment? We take that for granted here."

I stop for a moment to drain the bottle of water. I'm not leaning back in my chair anymore but right in their faces, explaining what I think is our only solution to prevent having to sell the colliders, the magnets, the auxiliary equipment, and all the other assets for scrap in two years and turn the miles of underground tunnels into artificially-lit shopping malls, fancy condominiums or—worst-case scenario—bunkers to protect us from World War III atomic bomb radiation.

"His team took the Golden Number [1] to a different level. They extruded the two-D model into three-D and called it the Golden Volume. The ratios maintained—the Fibonacci sequence flows through each assigned intersection like a maestro's fingers on a Stradivarius."

The men browse the books, seeming to stop only at pages displaying graphics and mathematical formulas in a quick peer review that could potentially find flaws and shake my confidence, but they remain silent.

The initial test passed, I continue, even more determined to drill into their skulls the now-or-never situation. "Look at how elegant that Fibonacci sequence is in the parallelepiped volume."

"Okay, I agree—they did something unique—but how can we apply it to what we do, which has a much higher degree of complexity?" Darren Mitten, the plum-bodied, red-haired American running SALVATION, intervenes to bring some convincing power to the team, still flipping back and forth through the book.

I can't sit anymore. I get up and resume pacing, my movement around the office forcing the men to shift in their chairs and their heads to follow me as if following a ball in a tennis match.

"There are millennia-old geometric shapes hiding more than we can possibly understand: the pyramid, the octahedron, and in my opinion, the rectangular parallelepiped formed by the Golden Number in which the Fibonacci Curve fits perfectly. It's the same ratio we find all around us in nature: sunflowers, shells, galaxies, pinecones—it's freaking unbelievable!" My voice is a note too high from the excitement.

I stop by the window, forcing the men to shift again. I have to spill all the beans now, building on their scientific interest. "What if we build a Fibonacci-type collider inside a Golden Volume structure? Any forth-grade kid knows that unusual processes, mainly positive ones, take place inside pyramids and octahedrons. What generates them? No one knows."

Silence. No more shuffling or fingering of the book.

I turn my back on them, pretending to peer at the horizon. Instead, I focus on their reflection in the window, giving them the pretense of privacy so they can whisper about the pros and cons of a concept coming from a guy who could never reach their level of scientific knowledge.

"Are you asking us to build a curved collider?" Chubuian asks, incredulous, his hands placed on the book on his knees. It's not a protective gesture—more of a demand for justification to spend money we don't have. "What do you expect out of it?"

I dread that question. I hope my improvised answer will be vague enough to satisfy them. If not, they'll do as I say anyway. They'll have to choose between working on this last attempt at salvation or a slow decay down the scientific community's memory lane.

"Expect the unexpected." I chuckle. "Maybe the particles don't have to travel at light speed in that geometric shape. Maybe there are internal energies and vibrations that do all the work, energies that can't be measured but are present at a more stable level. It's like the small eddy currents formed in the blood vessels. In an embryo, the blood is pumped and moved around before the heart is formed, so the notion that the heart's main purpose is to pump blood throughout our bodies is not completely true. It has help from these eddy currents. We might encounter a similar phenomenon in a Fibonacci-shaped collider," I say, ending most of my prepared speech.

"And you have no particular goal or thought on the potential outcome?" the head of SANCTUARY says, testing me again. He rubs his nose, itchy, no doubt, from the hair coming out of his left nostril. He does not take his eyes off me.

I'm pushing them around more than usual, and they want some guidance, so I decide to give in and confess. Maybe showing some goodwill on my part will help release some of theirs.

"I might have a hint about certain possibilities. I've done a bit of research, and I've even called Mircea Dacian. He's willing to join our team and give it a shot if you are also willing." I scratch my head and feel the annoying fatty bumps that have formed under the skin. They were not there before taking this job.

"Black hole. A miniature, insatiable black hole is what

we might get at the end of this exercise." I look at their faces, which are frozen in disbelief.

"Wow!"

It's a unanimous reaction, so I press on. "My suggestion is to insert the Golden Volume Fibonacci collider right after phase three of the acceleration process. Instead of injecting split particles into the LHC, release them into the Fibonacci, build a fair-sized collider wide enough for the vacuum tubes carrying the particles to fit in nicely," I say to ignite their appetite for crazy research. "It'll be trial-and-error to see which particles are prone to better results, their speed, and all the other spices that make life underground interesting."

I let them exchange statements too cryptic for me to understand. The positive energy appears to build inside them like those in the fired-up colliders.

"The Fibonacci spiral doesn't close on itself, so we'll have to build two such structures and unite their ends," Mitten announces loudly, his hairy hand leaning on the glass of my desk, exposing a tattoo in curvy letters, the name of a woman. "We need to fire particles using the same process we are using now but on a twisted trajectory and inside a ratio-perfect geometrical shape," Mitten explains in his lazy Louisianan accent.

I add another piece of significant information: "We've done so many tests on linear colliders with similar results. Time is still linear; there is no wrinkle that could open a portal to another dimension.

"Gentlemen, let me be very blunt: all those years ago, funding came to us like an avalanche in the Hautes-Alpes with a hidden goal. Somehow, the wild physics we're playing with through the collision of protons, neutrons, quarks, and the myriad other particles we keep unravelling will, in the end, rip a gate through the skin of this universe and into another one."

I stop again, open my small fridge loaded with bottles of water, and grab one. I'm about to shut the door when I realize I should offer some to the parched guys. It's a humanitarian gesture, especially since I am not done with them yet.

They consume the liquid in seconds.

"Portals to other universes? Are those guys totally insane?" Chubuian cries, his fingers nervously tearing at the label on the plastic bottle.

"I assure you, they are not. Science fiction movies have fallen behind the reality around us. Accessing a *Stargate*-type portal is only a matter of time, but it seems our funders have lost their patience. That's why I'm not trying to tweak existing processes but take a quantum leap into the unknown. We have nothing to lose," I say, maintaining an even level of enthusiasm in my voice. I'm beyond what I was allowed to offer as being forthcoming, but it's an executive decision I've had to make.

"We are playing with fire," Ivanciuk says, offering his two cents' worth, crossing his thick arms over his prominent chest. His eyebrows frown, and his eyes avoid mine as if my craziness could infect his mind through his retinas. "The general assumption is the black holes could be portals, but they could be anything else, too: another form of undiscovered energy floating in adjacent universes or a gargantuan vacuum cleaner that, once put in the ON position, won't stop until it sucks in every piece of matter out of the universe."

I don't react but think of a counter-argument intelligent enough to put his mind at ease. If he to an inoffensive home appliance, he's failed.

We all smirk.

I decide to ignore his remark and continue my own chain of thought, which is much more optimistic: "Maybe time bends in a Fibonacci Collider. Maybe, on impact, the particles behave in a way that triggers a similar excitation in a pair that collides at the same time in a parallel universe—entanglement at its best—and...bang," I clap my palms together, adding a sound effect that startles the men, "the portal appears.

"Before you object to what I've just said, please remember that even if I'm a scientist with good management skills, I do believe in the Universal Matrix binding all of us together. No matter how significant we think we are in the big scheme of things, geometry compels energy to flow in a specific way."

I'm done now. I've exhausted my entire ammunition and every one of my suggestions. My mental refuge is on the other side of the tinted windows, looking again at a sky that has frozen its clouds in photo-still positions. It feels like the Creator has held His breath for the duration of my passionate verbal outpouring.

Behind me, none of them speak, fumbling at the challenge I've thrown at them. It takes another long moment before Iurie Ivanciuk draws the conclusion I've been waiting for: "Okay. If there is no other logical path to saving our asses, we'll go with your strategy. We need about a month to determine, in theory, the optimal size for the two Fibonacci Colliders."

"Good luck," I say and keep staring at the beauty created by the universal, invisible energy while the men exit my office silently. The door closes behind them. Immediately, the clouds begin to sway again as they were waiting for the spectacle in my office to be over. I smile at my reflected image, but there is little satisfaction in having won the battle; the war still wages on in all of us.

* * *

At the end of the fourth day, after deliberating amongst themselves, Ivanciuk conveys the message to make arrangements for Dacian to come over. They won't start any significant work until the Romanian joins their ranks so everyone can start fresh on the venture. The researchers put aside their pride, eager to pick an outsider's brain. I'm not sure if they do it just to prove me wrong or out of fear that they might fail on their own. Regardless of their intention, I can't care less. I'm into water up to my chin, running an almost sunken ship, and left with barely enough time to say my prayers and salute the crew one more time, tears in my eyes.

Dacian arrives two weeks later. He's a tall, shiny-headed man, well-built if it weren't for the extra padding around his waist. He's a jovial fellow who smiles continuously and talks at an amazing speed, his mind like a Cray processor. It explains the publicly available long list of scientific papers, patents, innovations, and unaccountable ideas still waiting to be put into practice or taken over by research-hungry students. Even if he's humbled by the invitation to such a prestigious international facility, he doesn't seem overwhelmed.

His decades-long experience in chaos theory, complexity theory, geodynamics, and a myriad of other fields always seem to seamlessly interconnect in his mind, making him a perfect fit with the remaining team members.

I'm hosting all of them again in my office to hear the latest updates. "What are you going to use to build the

Golden Volume structure?" I ask, curious to see how the team has gelled after one week of working together.

Dacian tugs several times at his unshaven chin. I can practically see his mind flipping as it evaluates several options. "Bamboo," he says. This time, no smiling follows his statement.

No one lets out so much as a squeak, waiting for my reaction. I want to look smart, so I scramble for a question that might contest his selection. It comes out more as a concern than a serious inquiry that should give the Romanian scientist room to doubt himself. "Would it sustain that much weight?"

This time, it appears he can't hold back his smile anymore. "Hong Kong's skyscrapers were built using bamboo scaffolding. It's flexible, resistant, and most importantly, non-conductive. Make no mistake: the collider itself doesn't need any support. Its walls will be rigid enough to follow the Fibonacci curve. We use the bamboo to create the volume around it, similar to what the pyramid shape does to empty space. Building the collider without the structure determining the volume that, in turn, generates the unique properties is useless," Dacian explains, his words coming increasingly faster. He points to the three men standing quietly beside him. "We've already discussed that we'll have to rework the thickness of the walls, the materials they are made of, and the type of magnets that focus the beam. What we'll build is tiny compared to the twenty-seven kilometres the LHC has. It's a proof of concept, if you wish," Dacian concludes. He shifts his feet a couple of times in place, giving the impression he's ready to answer another tough question. Then, as an afterthought, he moves toward the whiteboard stuck on the wall to the right of my desk, grabs a black marker, and feverishly draws several circles of various sizes.

He turns toward the rest of us, his cheeks coloured by excitement, and pulls his long sleeves above his elbows, ready to lead me into the deeper scientific discussion they all had prior to arranging the meeting.

"We can't avoid using Phase One, where we strip the hydrogen atoms down to protons with a positive charge." He draws a checkmark in the smallest circle he's scribbled. "We also cannot bypass Phase Two¾the Booster Collider¾where we divide the initial pack of protons into four streams subjected to electric fields and electromagnets, or Phase Three¾the proton synchrotron." He points to the next two largest circles. "We need all of them to prepare the package with the right speed and weight," the Romanian says. He does a quick nod with his chin at Chubuian to indicate he should continue the presentation.

The Ukrainian's facial hair is still in disarray, but the entanglement is less pronounced, and it lacks the food grease he uses to give it a shiny twinkle. He takes the marker Dacian hands him like a baton in an athletic race and resumes the pitch. "The next two phases, the Super Proton Synchrotron (SPS) and the LHC, have to be eliminated and replaced by the FC," he says.

"FC?" I ask as the initials don't seem familiar.

"We named it the Fibonacci Collider. It's not feasible for us to build an FC that would match the SPS's length of seven kilometres. Based on our calculations, we can reach the Golden Volume after four iterations, giving us three times the length of the Booster, which is one hundred and fifty-seven meters. If the results show similarities to the ones in the LHC, then we could build a larger one. We know for a fact that the collider's spiral can't be kept on the same plane. It has to be built at a slight angle in order for the ends to connect properly." Chubuian puts all the details on the board, writing the lines so they cross the Fibonacci sequence, marking the angles and several formulas they used to reach this conclusion.

I measure up the scientists, waiting for my approval before going ahead with the plan. They were released of any responsibility the moment they accepted my change of direction. I was the one who'd earmarked the funds and who, in the end, will have to justify it in case of failure.

* * *

I'm in the control center surrounded by the entire team, ready to fire up the Fibonacci Collider. A year has passed since I agreed with how to build the FC. It was twelve stressful months during which I became an expert at making bogus excuses for the lack of the tangible results required in return for the money I kept requesting. Chubuian, standing on my right, takes over the discussion, animated by the fact that I'm on-site and eager to witness their accomplishments.

"As we said before, this is a proof of concept for a Golden Volume equivalent to only four iterations, so we don't need additional injection beam equipment to increase the energy along the way. We didn't go for a higher iteration number because Mircea shared another piece of his team's research with us, and we thought we could monitor that aspect as well," he says, taking a half-step backward to give Dacian the floor before bringing his sweaty hands together in a gesture of imminent prayer so misplaced in this facility, where not even God can enter without proper security clearance.

"Yes," the Romanian starts, his voice a little raspy, "we took the Golden Volume and generalized it for the nth dimension. We've come to the conclusion that our world is, in fact, part of a fourth-dimensional universe containing three other three-dimensional worlds, a "splinter," if you wish, of a much more complex and invisible volume. Our research highlights that the space created at the fourth iteration for the third dimension presents an interesting behaviour that doesn't replicate any further but could interact with other undetectable worlds. It's like a cry to the fourth dimension to come in and expand our reality by adding another degree of movement but not at the physical level. It's a more discreet plane, intangible, that we think has to do with the freedom of our minds through expanded consciousness. It's just a hint, but the added component is not Time, as we initially thought. Inside the bamboo structure, we've attached various sensors that feed into an application we've written to sense any time-space anomalies."

Dacian looks straight at me as if expecting me to categorize his idea as a new level of "crazy" above the one about the black hole. I disappoint him by shrugging my shoulders and showing my willingness to allow an exception to what we initially agreed upon.

Twenty cameras have been installed around the FC. I glance at the twisted metallic structure, lovingly embraced with bamboo poles. My mind skips back in time to when rollercoasters still ran on shaky wooden frames that squeaked and wailed with every passing cart full of screaming guests. I remember when I was one of those fools gratified by the cheap entertainment.

The snake of the Fibonacci Collider arches inward, as if looking to digest its own tail, only to find its twin sister firmly attached to its end, continuing its curvaceous form at an angle slightly different, as the researchers mentioned before. It's a beautiful sight, almost enough to make me cry —almost—but still, I'm proud of the team that didn't give up on my vision. Will it work? That is a question whose answer will be revealed shortly.

"Are we still injecting protons?" I ask just to be sure that nothing has changed since our last update two days ago and the excitement won't make them forget any procedural steps or record everything properly.

"Yes," Chubuian replies quickly. For a positive change, his blue T-shirt is clean, and his beard is groomed. A broad smile parts his facial hair. Confidence exudes from everyone crowded around the control board. I switch from one video camera to another, checking each angle. The impromptu space for delivering the latest addition to CERN's technological wizardry has to be close enough to the proton synchrotron for the two of them to connect and exchange the charged protons. Thick packs of wires sneak into both ends of the collider, pinned down by duct tape and tool carts with open drawers, showing their contents. Leftover metal pipes and tubes are piled in a mish-mash in one corner from the clean-up before the test. Neon lights hang from the high ceiling; the light reaches the floor as delicately as the morning dew.

There is no more sign of Mr. Woo and his son, the specialists who built the bamboo frame. Their job is done; they have long since been packed up and parcelled back to Hong Kong. This was the weirdest contract by far, Mr. Woo had told Dacian. The men had formed an instant connection due to a certain happiness and openness by which they both lived their lives.

I look up to assess the dimensions of the Golden Volume's four iterations Ivanciuk mentioned, forcing my neck to strain its muscles, still sour after my overzealous gym training. I can't hold back a grimace, thinking about how inept the situation is: unleashed technology bringing most of Earth's natural balance to the brink of destruction; nevertheless, Nature still offers us a hand in a gesture of reconciliation, having provided the bamboo. The men and women making up the limited team fret around me, anxious to punch in the keys to select the first test case, mixed with the euphoria of anticipating that what follows will be a successful and unheard-of scientific challenge.

"We'll kick them at the maximum designed energy: seven TeV[2]," Ivanciuk says. He immediately clears his throat as if to bring my attention to the task at hand.

I gather my strained thoughts and focus on his mouth as the words come out slowly, like puffs of smoke from the mouth of a smoker. "We've run several simulations on how much energy the protons can gain between the release and the point of contact." He stops for a moment and nods to Mitten, who quickly moves the mouse on the black mouse pad marked with CERN's logo. The movement brings up the results of one of the simulations Iurie Ivanciuk just mentioned on the monitor.

"As you can see," he points his index finger at the swirling red, green, and blue lines generating havoc between the two horizontal lines delineating the safety zone, "we are shooting blanks. Our historical data is all based on a linear trajectory that behaves like a well-trained pet. Most of the time, you can guess the outcome, but not in this case." The Ukrainian stares at the monitor as if hoping some hidden code or other will materialize at the precipice of the experiment.

"Are you saying you can't train the particles to behave

on a twisted trajectory?" I ask, a bit concerned about the inconclusiveness of the computer models.

There is a deep silence disturbed only by the soles of shoes rubbing on the carpet.

It's Dacian's turn to salvage the team's pride. "Look, indeed, we can't say, one hundred percent, how these puppies will perform inside the collider, but we'll treat them gently. Just a bit of a touch to be sure the magnets will keep them in the middle of the vacuum tubes, straight and safe like pearls on a string.

"What Iurie means to say is that speed is something we can control, but the energy they are going to accumulate along the way, we can't. That's the worrisome part," he says, still staring at the same results on the monitor. "As in the LHC, we'll run the protons counterclockwise in the vacuum tubes, but because of the unusual path, we can't predict if some of them will lose speed and 'be late' on impact, generating unpredictable results." Dacian's voice is seemingly devoid of any trace of confidence.

I dig my hands into my side pockets while gazing at the monitor image of the bamboo structure weaved in perfect geometric symmetry I'm not having second thoughts about pushing the levers myself if need be; it is just the anguish of this unexpected energy component that makes the research invaluable. It's morale-damaging to show indecisiveness in front of the team, but my lips feel glued together, I can't taste anything, my teeth are clenched, and my back muscles tense and ready to rip through my Italian-made cotton shirt. Everyone is tired. Dark bags hang beneath their eyes, their cheeks sucked in from sleepless nights, irregular meals, and too-many-to-count mugs of coffee. They all want to be done with this, successful or not. I want to send them home for a couple of days then have them back to run the test, but I know they'll revolt and shut me down, no matter if I'm the boss.

"Let's do it," I say and follow it with a mental prayer.

* * *

In the void that follows, God's voice thunders, annoyed: "Now, I'll have to rebuild this world again. Another demanding six days of creating humans and the rules they have to live by, only now, they are prepared to experience an upgraded cycle in which science and spirituality have to co-exist. That's the only way to bring them back to me forever, safely on a higher astral plane."

[1] In mathematics, two quantities are in the *golden ratio* if their ratio is the same as the ratio of their sum to the larger of the two quantities. It is also known as the Fibonacci sequence.

[2] TeV - Tera electron Volt

Chapter 8

Crystal Continuum

The priest in charge of Daniel's baptism was the black sheep of the Church. In the past, there had been some complaints about his unorthodox ways of interpreting the Holy Book. There were also concerns regarding the customs and rituals on display for the appeasement and self-reassurance of those still attending Sunday mass and the myriad of smaller religious weekly celebrations.

In the Normies' eyes, such gestures were more sacrilegious than the innuendo that the priest had had an affair with a socially respected woman or young lad. Somehow, the mere suggestion of deviant behaviour in one's past sent everyone's consciousness into mental somersaults until it became a de facto reality.

High-ranking investigations into these complaints cleared the priest. No one knew if he had connections in those high places or if the Church was on another leg of transformation from within. This time, perhaps it would sway toward leniency.

On that fall day, when Daniel became a member of the

blessed family, Father Dimitrie had the instinct—or maybe it was divine guidance—to add even more awkwardness to the list previously compiled by his detractors.

He materialized a pointy, ten-inch hexagonal-shaped quartz crystal from the folds of his brocaded robes just before submerging it in the lukewarm water waiting for him in the copper bowl as it rested on its wooden legs.

Daniel's parents—young and intimidated by the priest's baritone voice as it bounced off the walls depicting angels, holy men with golden auras around their heads enacting allegoric scenes from the same book the priest was reading—would relinquish any control over what the representative of the clergy might do to the boy. As second-generation immigrants, for them, the Church was where you went for weddings and baptisms, and it was a bit overwhelming overall.

"In the name of the Father, the Son, and the Holy Spirit, I bless this child to become a pillar of the community, a clarion call heard and followed by many." The priest cleared his throat and placed the crystal in the tiny hands that grabbed it as tightly as if it were a lifeline. Daniel didn't squirm or wriggle as the cleric's right arm embraced his body like a tentacle while the left hand gently clamped his nostrils together.

One…two…three, and the boy was awash in the holy water, not to mention imbued with the crystal's vibrations.

Daniel squeaked in lieu of his acceptance of this landmark in his life. His godmother, a plump forty-something red-haired woman, rushed toward him, a puffy towel hung over her extended arms, ready to welcome the boy, comfort him, and dress him in white silk pants, a brocaded jacket, and miniature white leather shoes. Days later, the garb would be returned to the young family as a memento of the day.

"Father, Daniel won't release the crystal," his godmother said apologetically. Tears of happiness had left black marks on her cheeks, turning her into the perfect embodiment of another famous religious celebration from a distant country: the Day of the Dead.

"No need to take it away. It is his to use and protect," the priest said with a smug smile. "Let him hold it for a while. He won't hurt himself."

"Does it have a particular meaning?" the boy's father asked, scratching his right ear from which hung an ouroboros-like silver ring. His kempt beard, combed hair, and suit, even with its worn-out patches, gave the priest a good vibe.

"Yes, it has meaning for him. In fact, he will discover its purpose when he gets older; just don't hide it away. I see Daniel standing tall in front of others, living by example, giving hope."

The young man nodded.

The family and guests left the church, on their way to gorge themselves at a Mandarin restaurant nearby.

Liliana's face had mesmerized Daniel since grade five. He wasn't aware of the concept of love at first sight, so he treated the wave of heat and obsession he felt with her as a curiosity.

She had arrived as a new student from a corner of the country he'd never heard of, but when the teacher introduced her, the sound of the word—Miami—had a flare of aristocracy about it, an air of happiness that, for whatever reason, made him happy, too.

The quartz crystal entrusted to him at his baptism had turned him into a crystal enthusiast of sorts. It was the lens through which he perceived the world around him. He noticed the emeralds where Liliana's eyes should be, implying a tendency toward balance, wisdom, and patience. The contour of her face was a perfectly chiselled, round selenite that had retained a miniature slit, where a carnelian was a placeholder for her mouth. He liked the colour and stone combination so much that he decided to make Liliana a close friend. That she did, indeed, become, but instead of becoming one fully immersed in his marvellous world of crystals, she wore them.

In grade eight, when his hormones affected blood fluctuations, Daniel could barely control himself when Liliana was close by, and the relationship flared. They were vulnerable and eager to know each other, and they associated their most intimate body parts with known crystals. Daniel had his list and Liliana hers, developed with Daniel's help of course.

"Do you really believe cave crystals could create a wrinkle in time, even when submersed in water?" Liliana asked several days after he'd shared an article from an old issue of *National Geographic* focusing on the gigantic quartz crystals in the Naica Cave in Chihuahua, Mexico.

"Anything is possible. Either they grew in that environment over thousands of years or there was a glitch in one of the parallel timelines, intentional or not, that made them manifest in our dimension," Daniel said, unwilling to ask what sparked the sudden interest in the sunken treasures. He looked at her with gratitude for bringing up the one subject he never tired of talking about.

"There is no active energy portal at that location and no disappearances have been reported, just high levels of ionized air," Daniel said. The discussion stopped there, with Liliana caressing the quartz gifted to her by her lover.

Months later, on a summer day, between hugging and kissing while lying on a blanket on the patch of forest edging the suburb, Daniel flung his heart wide open and finally decided to share the story of his most precious possession. He pulled the quartz from his backpack, held it up to the sun, and frowned at it through the branches of light, which broke into a series of rainbows. Daniel felt its vibration, a language he had only recently begun to fully understand.

"Touch it," he encouraged Liliana, his hand covering hers. "It's magnificent!" he said, and then he blacked out.

* * *

Daniel awoke, still holding the quartz in both hands. He looked down to see his skin had taken on a darker cast, and his nails had grown longer and slimmer. They were done up in a light blue, resembling agate stone, one of his favourites.

He leaned against a pillow against an unfamiliar, rich headboard. Creamy silk sheets folded over a comforter depicted fractal patterns, allowing the reality of the situation to bleed through his persistent headache.

The heaviness on his chest attracted his attention, where breasts of perfectly geometric, sensual amber crystals sat. They resembled Liliana's only fuller and of a much brighter hue than Liliana's. Were they a fair trade for hers?

There was no nearby reflective surface that might have shown him more of his new-found physical reality without leaving the bed and potentially exposing more of his naked body.

One hand released the quartz and carefully lifted the edge of the blanket, bringing some light into the dark place. He brought his head closer to the gap between the blanket and the mattress.

"Gee whiz!" he hissed, sounding like air escaping a pressurized pipe.

He dropped the edge of the comforter and froze—the emerald between his legs that had grown larger with age, and the quality of which he was proud was gone.

Liliana!

He looked to his left, hoping to find her crystal body he adored.

There laid a body, but it was not hers—unless she'd also suffered as radical a transformation as his own. He saw a man sleeping on his belly, his wide back exposed and covered in fractal tattoos similar to the ones on the comforter. They pulsed lightly in synch with the man's breath. On his bald head was a square patch of a slightly different colour, inviting a tug from inquisitive fingers. Daniel didn't dare touch it.

He tried hard to associate any of the man's body parts with crystals but failed.

"Not my time. Not my place," he muttered. "Where am I?"

The man moved slightly and turned toward him, eyes closed. He wore a beard and had a crooked nose.

Slowly, in spite of his good judgement not to leave the bed naked, he inched out from under the comforter with small moves. The floor was pleasantly warm.

He took two quick steps to the floor-to-ceiling window at the side of his bed, which let in a faint luminosity. He touched it as if half-expecting it to bite off his finger. Instead, the window talked back to him with a feminine lilt: "What level of opacity would you prefer, Juliana? The usual?"

Daniel panicked upon hearing "the usual." He couldn't awaken by whatever level of light the smart window would let in, so he improvised: "Fifty percent of the usual," he said, hoping to get a peek outside. The glass panel at eye level changed polarization, but the view was blurry. With another whisper, he adjusted it, maintaining the dim ambient light.

He was in a skyscraper, high above the surrounding buildings. There wasn't a single speck of green in sight other than the tiny parks and gardens lost within the forest of glass structures that stretched to the horizon.

Overcast weather brought gloominess to the scenery. The city was predominately grey, the only colours were those on the billboards integrated into several building facades. He squinted, trying to make out the ads in an attempt to place a date and time on his new and inexplicable identity.

Upgrade to the latest 10 TB implants. Find the nearest location or book online. Our technicians will come to you. In the ad, a woman in her twenties stared into the camera. She turned to show her profile, and a robotic arm removed a patch of skin on her otherwise bald scalp. The angle changed again, showing what was resting beneath it: a microchip the size of his pinky nail. The robotic arm removed the chip with ease and replaced it with a similar chip depicting the same red and white letter S. The second chip purportedly held a higher data capacity.

He wondered if they'd really gone toward transhumanism, and if so, what was the guy's capacity was. Had he upgraded?

He focused on another ad that seemed to link several floors on different buildings into a uniform structure. "Mars is open for farming," it said. "Locusts, ants, worms. Guaranteed government subsidies and thirty-year low interest rates. One-way trip only." The side of the billboard showed a three-D rendering of the existing Mars habitat, its low-rise structures connected in various configurations for easy access between buildings. Departure dates flickered beneath it in large characters. "January 01, 2055. Celebrate New Year's in space," it said.

It still didn't help to frame the time slot into which he'd found himself thrown. It was like living in one of those time-travel novels he'd devoured when younger, but it wasn't at all fun having to do it in the body of a naked woman at the disposal of a fractally bulky man Daniel knew nothing about.

The shuffle of bed sheets rattled him. He hushed the window into full polarization, then slipped back into bed, his mind propelled to the highest processing speed possible.

"Honey, are you okay? It's my turn to please you, now," the man said, shifting his weight closer.

Panic shredded Daniel's insides.

"What's wrong, honey?" He moved closer, his shovel-like hands grabbing Daniel's left amber and squeezing it gently. Daniel squeaked like a mouse about to die of a heart attack upon the approach of a cat.

Maybe it was intuition or the quartz coordinating his thoughts, but he placed the crystal in the man's hands. He put his on top, screamed, "It's magnificent!" and blacked out.

* * *

Daniel felt as stiff as a crystal rod. He couldn't move, nor could he open his eyes. The paralysis scared him more than the tattooed man from his last jump. If he had no way to escape the man's embrace—not to mention whatever romantic activity he planned to continue—Daniel could feign enjoyment.

Liliana had once told him that women faked pleasure during intercourse. There were benefits in that, whether in marriage or the occasional fling. Daniel couldn't wrap his mind around the sham behaviour, and he'd asked the girl if she'd ever done it with him. She'd denied it, and he'd believed her, too much in love with the angles of light playing on her selenite body to care.

He was out in the open somewhere, surrounded by trees moving back and forth in the tender wind as it whispered through them. Daniel hoped to hear human voices approaching so he could ask for help. Skipping across time-lines without notice or preparation had begun to annoy him more than being unable to associate people and things with crystals.

Was it the quartz's frequency that initiated his adventure? How many jumps would there be before he returned home? No one would ever believe what he'd gone through except maybe Liliana.

Maybe.

A flicker of light penetrated the darkness. His eyes slowly adjusted as the brightness increased. "Whoa!" he said when he realized his surroundings.

He was in a tree way up high, towering over the entire forest. The ground was not visible, hidden as it was by leafy branches reaching out in all directions.

"Welcome home," he heard someone's greetings.

Daniel moved just his eyes; no other parts of his body seemed mobile.

"Elder, so glad to have you back."

He couldn't see the entity addressing him.

"Your soul left us, saddened, as it was, by our brothers' destruction. We were so worried about you."

An American dipper landed on a branch at eye level, distracting him. Its faint grey feathers and happy chirping filled him with joy. *A river must be nearby*, he thought, and he pricked his ears, searching for the sound of running water. *How do I know what type of bird it is? How do I know it likes to dip in the water?*

In front of him, the lower trees seemed to lean toward him, bowing in a way the light wind couldn't manifest.

"You are still unsure of where you are," the voice addressed him again.

He frowned, but he couldn't feel his eyebrows. "Who are you?" he shot back, not expecting an answer but still defiant, regardless of his immobile and vulnerable position.

"We are you. We are the forest." The reply came cloaked in the leaves that surrounded him like the sea.

He breathed in, and sap propelled to the tips of his fingers, tickling and refreshing them at the same time. "Where is my quartz?" he asked, dismissing the previous answer as unreliable, nothing more than a figment of his imagination.

He couldn't bring his hands together, but he somehow knew there was no hexagonal object in either of them.

"It is buried deep under your roots. It is the crystal that gave you the energy and potency to become our Elder."

Daniel heard an echo of confirmation reverberate

through the entire forest. Branches and leaves touched, amplifying their consent.

"We all get lost at some point in our growing process," the forest's voice assured him. "It's the strength of the community that always brings us back."

Daniel straightened his gaze. A mountain range tipped with a snow canopy made an utterly fantastic, powerful view. In the life where Liliana and crystals had been his main focus, he'd wanted a treehouse with shelves to hold his crystals, sorted by colour and property. He couldn't have one in the building where his family lived. He smiled—at least, he thought he did; he had become a treehouse.

Elder Daniel swayed his slim body several times as if shaking off the memory of living in other universes. He was reassuringly back, his roots entrenched in the fertile soil, feeling everyone pulse, be they seedlings or mature trees. Relinquishing the Elder's position had been a hollow proposition.

The forest needed his strength, his vantage point, and last but not least, the wisdom encrypted in the quartz beneath him.

The horizon turned scarlet. "It's magnificent!" was the message he sent to the forest, only this time, his eyes remained glued to the defiant beauty of spirit that everyone saw through him.

Chapter 9

The Story of the Seven Lakes

The Story of the Seven Lakes surrounding the peaks of the Sacred Mountain had immemorial roots. Word-of-mouth surviving generations now extinct said that God created Adam and Eve as giants and this was the place they first walked as living beings. The heaviness of their bodies left deep recesses on the moist soil that later filled with the Water God used to bless the land after His important creation.

Shaken by the awareness of who they were, Adam and Eve knelt down, faced each other, and pushed up the ground that was now the Sacred Mountain, but only Adam's left knee touched the ground. The other helped him to keep his footing, pressing hard for balance. Adam's Right Foot Lake is the deepest, and some say the most treacherous.

The mountain's dizzying heights and jagged edges have never been conquered by mortal climbers on their way to fame. Over the millennia, humans learned to stay away for their own safety, gazing at the threatening peaks from a distance while satisfying their daily fulfilment of mundane tasks.

Word had it that the wisdom and lessons transmitted by the gurus and yogis in these communities were far more knowledgeable than any wisdom or lessons found in the printed word.

Stories rolled into myths like timid mounds of snow that, when reaching their tipping point, became devastating avalanches. The few individuals touched by the teachings neither confirmed nor denied the validity of the primordial creation nor what happened after Adam and Eve, mesmerized by the love beaming from their physical shell, did.

How could love and the realization that they were spirit moulded into physicality, shrunk to a size, and allowed to procreate for nimble integration into what they understood to be Mother? Why had Adam and Eve kept to themselves the knowledge about the healing powers of their tears that, when stored in vials even as small as a thimble, could bring health and prosperity to humanity as a whole? Was it true that God had imprinted the Water of the Lakes with innate intelligence and awareness as a fluid vigilante over humankind? Historians had yet to uncover any written word about Water's role in the creation of Adam, Eve, or any of their descendants, for that matter.

A trickle of whispering water found its way down the slopes, maneuvering around stones and fallen logs and clearing layers of fallen leaves to come to rest in a clear puddle at the end of its arduous journey. Humans and animals alike quenched their thirst from these liquid veins traversing Mother in all directions, but only a handful of them appreciated the gift of life through open prayers and thankful thoughts.

Centuries passed before inquisitive minds acknowledged the omnipresence and potency of Water. She played so many characters at once: fluid in the shape of the oceans, rivers, and ponds; vapour in a state of humidity and flying rivers; solid in the monumental ice sculptures on the sides of unforgiving steep mountains and aged icecaps. Over time, the spiritual and scientific inquiries stirred in a cauldron of evolutionary thinking to raise the unthinkable question: was Water another form of God?

Heads nodded or shook in equal measure. Were they afraid to elevate Water to such an inconceivable level? Was it a sacrilege?

But Water seemed to know it all, having recorded the rise and fall of life on Earth from its inception in its fluid molecular structure. This, naturally, begged another query to be dropped into the pool of human consciousness: if the awakened Water seeped down from the Sacred Mountain, did it contain traces of Adam and Eve's biological imprints?

People's thoughts scattered in all directions like a beehive under a bear attack, appalled by the subtle intention Water sent to them, suggesting them discover the bond between Herself and God.

Is Water another aspect of God?

The mystery remains unsolved.

Chapter 10

Streams of Consciousness

These are thoughts and concepts that appear in my mind during long meditations. I hope each of you will resonate with certain paragraphs.

(1) - Inner Child

I never put too much thought into the Inner Child concept, let alone into healing it from a potential past trauma. The trauma didn't happen to us, right?

The times we are living through, times of intense energy cleansing and ascension, require a deeper introspection into this aspect of ourselves.

The revelation is that what is hidden behind our emotional gates are actions of the past that crumbled and wrinkled our innocence and were embedded in us at the time of birth by Divine law. The older we get, the smaller and more frightened our Inner Child becomes to form a wimpy image of our true essence.

The yelling of a mad and impatient parent, a slap from an abusive uncle, and the feeling of emptiness when a family separation occurs, shrinks the Inner Child even more, puts it into a tiny but hardened box where feelings lose their meaning, lose their real names, and forget they belong to the surface where they are attached to a wonderful, loving, thriving human being.

Like in a movie, the Inner Child becomes evidence of a crime, sunken into the bottomless lake of the subconscious, never to be retrieved.

Sometimes, a Divine, guided spark of love and light ignites our heart back into the memory, retrieving such a priceless part of ourselves. This jolt can be powerful and induce enough energy to shake the box, pulverize its lock, and bring its contents to the surface again.

It's a victory against all odds.

(2) - Ego Dump

What some call an Ego Dump, I equate with a scream on paper, where only the lined white surface is scarred, taking in all the pain and frustration of life up to that moment on top of unresolved memory fragments from previous lives.

This silent dump might not be as efficient as a jagged roar of desperation and liberation in the forgiving silence of the forest or in an open field, but it will liberate the physical avatar of the enormous pressure encapsulated by social norms, cultural customs, or beliefs that never resonated with us.

When in time do we start the Ego Dump exercise if we've never done it before? At three years old, when we realize, for the first time, that there is a world around us? Or a bit later, after the identification of family members, their rank on the food chain, and who is friendlier or less predisposed to give in to tantrum sessions?

It's hard to decide. At that age, innocent and without expectations, one doesn't know rules or labels such as abuse and kindness. One only knows unconditional love from inside the womb and beyond, and the Inner Child will accept nothing less.

But what if society at large has no idea of such a concept? What if even a single derisive remark, even in passing, is enough to counteract the Ego Dump process?

The Inner Child is relevant in a societal structure built for a "fight-or-flight" mentality.

What if adults perceive their actions and tools to strengthen character, teach lessons, and create able bodies that later add to the family's chance of survival and perpetuation? What if the children cannot forget the abuse and trauma?

Forgiveness is achievable, but letting go and healing wounds take time.

How many of us forgive and heal before passing the baton to our own children, perpetuating the emotional abyss along with the health and psychological implications?

(3)

The Love for God keeps one's heart on a wide river connecting Him with the ocean, with the energy of all. Choosing the opposite of Love is like navigating a narrow stream toward a dead end.

There is no satisfaction floating on such perilous waters, where the danger of being stranded in an inhospitable land is always present.

Only the Love of God is protective, permissive, and reassuring that all is going to be fine, no matter the imminent and short-lived turbulence.

Love brings Light with it, and Light is accompanied by Gratitude for the notion that of the Creator.

We are such amazing sparkles of energy, and we don't realize it. We enjoy putting ourselves down at the first sign of weakness. We betray the sacred within, choosing an easy path of self-loathing, pity, and ate, and any feelings that push our sails deeper into the narrow and shallow dead-end stream.

Awakening is not easy, but it is achievable. One thought alone, "Thank you, God," is woven into the feeling of unconditional Love, and it keeps our rudders in the middle of the river leading toward the ocean of indescribable happiness.

Once you arrive in those waters, the danger of relapsing vanishes. Temptations, undesirable relationships, traumas, and any traces of energetic dirt have been cleansed to be as pure as God desires.

We are who we are and nothing less. Open your eyes to the new YOU! Be impressed by your potential.

Be impressed by your desire to Love and be in service. This is who YOU are!

(4)

The phrase "Know thyself" comes from the Greeks, but I think the statement is much, much older. Maybe it has to do with the origins of Creation.

God knew He had powers, but he had not previously had the chance to test the limits of His power or the limits of His imagination. He started to experiment by creating matter, hence knowing Himself through His creations.

We can see and feel that His imagination has no boundaries. If we imagine something, it means it already existed somewhere in the fabric of this dimension or in a higher one, in the fabric of this timeline or in a parallel one.

This is my own explanation for everything that comes into existence and is still being created as we speak.

(5)

I am the sword of Light, cutting through the thickness of forgetfulness. Back and forth, back and forth; the cut gets deeper and wider.

What is left are fog-free, objective remains, hidden from many of us over countless lives.

(6)

I am the vapour rising from a mighty waterfall, gaining perspective of the world beneath me, busy and indifferent to the life I carry within me.

I sustain a fertile womb that will burst with energy at the place that needs it most: a patch of cultivated land whose withering plants cry of thirst; a sliver of forest whose roots cannot reach underground water reserves; or an almost bone-dry lake on which animals' survival depends.

I am everything you need: humble in how I handle myself but mighty and unapologetic when my messages are disregarded.

I am your dearest friend and fiercest enemy at the same time.

I am the lover who caresses without expectation, the fist that smashes rock; I am humanity's memory.

I carry the energy of Mother Earth, the vibration of far-away constellations and interplanetary dust.

My molecule is encrypted for the uninitiated while wide open to the Creator.

You, searching soul, want to unlock my secrets?

Merge with that omnipotent energy that creates all, including me. That's the highest challenge for you. I am You, and You are Me.

In school, you were taught that water makes up 70% or more of your physical composition. If my state of being within you is not in balance, you will feel it.

Your intention to get well can heal me, and thus, heal You. You are your own healer. Bring me to a state of harmony and joy. Structure me into the shape of a beautiful hexagon, and I'll become the fiddle on which you can play the notes of a harmonious life.

I am omnipresent; I am another aspect of God.

About the Author

Claudiu Murgan is enthralled by human consciousness and the notion of our place in the enormous wheels of the Multiverse. His settings in science fiction, fantasy, or eco-fiction focus on describing the beauty of Mother Nature who demands action from all of us.

He has called Canada home since 1997 when he immigrated from Romania.

He authored three fiction novels that were translated into the Romanian language. Claudiu's short stories were published in anthologies in the USA, Canada, Italy, and Romania.

He is the host of the Spiritually Inspired podcast that brings inspiration and guidance to those searching for the spiritual aspect of their life.

- www.ClaudiuMurgan.com
- www.SpirituallyInspired.ca
- www.GnosticTV.com/programs/claudiu-murgan

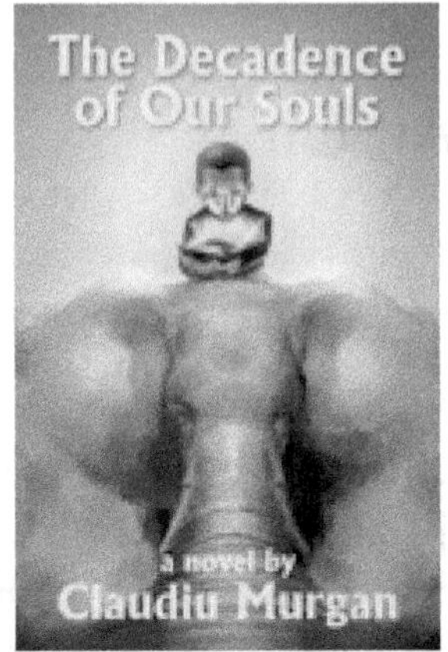

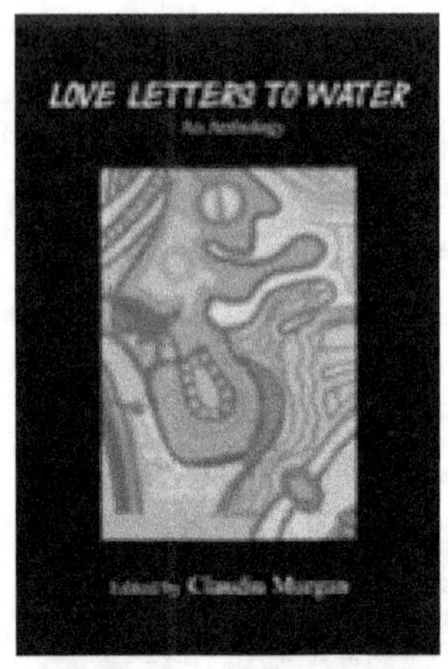

The audio versions are on Audible.com / Audible.ca

 facebook.com/ClaudiuMurganAuthor

 x.com/ClaudiuMurgan

instagram.com/claudiumurgan